Faith, Hope & Chastity

James Henry Tait

Grosvenor House
Publishing Limited

This book is published by
Grosvenor House Publishing Ltd
Link House
140 The Broadway, Tolworth, Surrey, KT6 7HT.
www.grosvenorhousepublishing.co.uk

A CIP record for this book
is available from the British Library

Paperback ISBN 978-1-80381-542-8
Hardback ISBN 978-1-80381-543-5
eBook ISBN 978-1-80381-544-2

Dedication

To the memory of my dearest wife, who loved and supported me throughout our courtship and marriage in all my endeavours and blessed me with the legacy of four caring and loving daughters who have made the rest of my life worth living. My thanks, too, to all my grandchildren and great-grandchildren for the treasure of their smiles and happy laughter.

My appreciation to my publishers for their commitment to successfully undertake the publication of this book despite all the challenges I gave them.

About the Author

Former magazine editor and writer of fiction, non-fiction and verse. Born 1930 in Dulwich south London England of working-class parents.

Motherless at twenty months. Lived with grandparents in the deprived Thameside area of Bermondsey until his father remarried in 1934. Evacuated to South Wales at the outbreak of war in 1939. Qualified for grammar school education in 1941; returned to London on the death of his father in 1944. Made homeless twice as a result of enemy V1 and V2 rocket air attacks. Left school in 1946 and worked briefly in a City of London office before joining the Merchant Navy, serving on cargo freighters to European and Mediterranean ports before joining the Royal Air Force in 1950. Began his writing career with the founding of his squadron's magazine, writing articles and editing contributions from serving members until leaving the service in 1962. During this 12year period he married and became the father of four daughters. On demob, found civilian employment with a life Insurance company, combining those duties with writing short stories and editing a monthly magazine for former pupils of his grammar school. That hobby ended with the death of his wife in 2008. Retired and wrote his autobiography, One Day At A Time, two volumes of personal verse and a crime novel. This present book, Faith, Hope and Chastity is his swansong.

Chapter 1

Jean Stanley thrust her primary school pupils' exercise books into her well-worn leather satchel, took a final look around the classroom and closed the door firmly behind her. It was Friday, the end of her working week apart from the correcting and marking of the English essays, which she could do at home.

It was beginning to drizzle as she crossed the playground, turned left outside the wrought iron gates and headed for the bus stop. A few of her form pupils were still gathered in a chattering group on the pavement discussing their weekend arrangements. They opened rank to let her pass, and a piping chorus of "Good night, Miss Stanley" followed her up the hill. She smiled and waved a hand in acknowledgement. As she did so, the parish church chimed the hour of 4pm.

Overhead, the cumulous cloud was thickening, darkening the grey street and casting a shadow like a dirty thumbprint over Bucton Tor. The mountain rose like a camel's hump above the village, dominating the landscape. Jean thought of her father working in the site hut on the lip of the limestone quarry and wondered if he still remembered the promise that he had made at breakfast to drive her to the committee meeting at the village hall that evening. She had been wheedled into becoming the treasurer of the local community association, and with the annual autumn dance event only two weeks away, the committee awaited her report of the accounts.

Jean pursed her lips and frowned. It was with a degree of frustration that she had received the notification from her repair garage that her vehicle needed a new clutch and would not be available for use until the following Monday. She had promised her mother that she would return her library books to Punting town library and collect two more in exchange, and she had also booked a hairdressing appointment at the local salon. It had momentarily occurred to her to ask Ben to drive her to both venues, knowing that he would have jumped at the chance of escorting her, but she had not seen him for several weeks, and she did not want to encourage any false hopes he may still have.

Standing at the bus stop holding an umbrella and the satchel, Jean let her mind slip back to the time when she and Ben had been constant companions. She smiled at the memory. How simple life seems when you are very young! She and Ben had grown up in neighbouring houses, and they had laughed and romped together in the meadow beside the river that ran through the village. They had even learned to swim in the calm water below the weir. In the summer, they often skinny-dipped without costumes, unembarrassed and unashamed of their nascent bodies as they tumbled and swam in the slow-running tributary. That period of gleeful, innocent behaviour came to an end when they were observed by the local busybody Maisie Parsons from the shelter of blackthorn bushes.

Maisie was the local postmistress who made it her business to know everybody else's business. There was not a young girl in the village that discovering herself pregnant out of wedlock could hope to conceal her indiscretion from Maisie. She knew of all impending births, marriages and deaths (hatches, matches and dispatches as the jovial Reverend Geoffrey Simpson irreverently termed these natural events) and what scandalous facts she did not know she invented. She accused Ben and Jean of behaving indecently. The two youngsters were scarcely aware of the charge against them but vehemently denied any wrongdoing. When Maisie had finished her tirade, the children turned and ran, Ben hot-faced; Jean trying to stop the sobs in her throat. She wanted to report the matter to her mother but in the end said nothing. She and Ben eventually found a secluded spot further downriver, but the virginal pleasure they had previously enjoyed had been tainted by the charge of licentious behaviour. Skinny dipping became a pleasure of the past long before puberty made them aware of their sexuality.

Chapter 2

It was with relief that Jean caught sight of the Punting bus trundling down the hill towards her. She tightened her grip on her satchel as she climbed aboard and took her seat. The rain was falling more heavily, obscuring her view out of the window. It would be at least half an hour before she arrived at the stop outside the library. She paid her fare and relaxed back against the cloth-cushioned seat. The weather reminded her of the day she had returned from teaching college. She had caught the late afternoon train from London, and it was pouring with rain when she alighted at Punting station.

Ben was standing on the platform waiting to greet her. She was pleased to see him but was shocked by his appearance. In the three years since she had been away studying for her diploma, he seemed to have shrunk. He greeted her eagerly, and the grip on her arm as he escorted her from the station seemed to burn through her clothing. Driving her back to her home, he plied her with incessant questions as if he needed to draw sustenance from her responses. He seemed to have become dehydrated from lack of contact with her, though they had regularly corresponded. She answered his questions willingly enough, but for the first time in her life, she felt an undefinable sense of unease with him.

That night, lying in the still darkness of her bed, she thought again about him, trying to analyse her feelings. Until she had gone off to college, Ben had been, apart from her father, the predominate male figure in her life. Yet, in her innocence, his gender was inconsequential in their relationship. Their friendship had been nonphysical, uninhibited by sexual connotations. Of course, there had been spontaneous kisses at times, born from

4

wit or gaiety but accomplished with complete ingenuousness. Or so Jean had thought. Looking back, she was surprised by her own naivety, remembering the odd unguarded moments when she had caught Ben's gaze on her: his eyes aflame with such intensity that she had wondered what hidden torture lay behind them. His eventual confession of deep love, accompanied by a proposal of marriage, caught her completely by surprise. She had considered him the deepest of friends but had never held any yearning for a more passionate attachment. They had often discussed their hopes for the future, and Ben had known of her ambition to go to university and become a teacher. Marriage at an early age was not part of her plans; dreams of romance were submerged under career ambitions.

She tried to let Ben down gently. She explained her feelings: how important his friendship was, how much she cared for him, but she had set her heart on teaching and marriage to Ben or anybody else lay far on a distant horizon. Ben was disconsolate, despite Jean's kiss on his cheek, and took himself off with the eagerness gone from his eyes. Jean did not see him for several days but heard that he had spent most of his time drowning his sorrows in the local inn. When she finally caught up with him and expressed her concern, he had looked at her with a heavy frown and muttered that he understood. He wished her well, but it was better that they did not see each other. He talked about finding work on the other side of town. Jean nodded and let him go. She did not see him again before she left home for university.

Jean aroused from her sad recollections and shivered as the bus began its descent into Punting town centre. She pulled her coat close around her, picked up her satchel and umbrella and prepared to alight. It was dark now, the lights in the main street hazy with rain. As the bus ground to a halt outside the library, Jean manoeuvred her way to the door and stepped onto the pavement, carefully avoiding the stream that ran down the gutter. The flagstones glistened wetly as she walked up the steps to the library entrance. She was greeted at the reception desk by a smiling Sheila. Jean placed her mother's loaned books on the counter.

"Hullo, Sheila. I am in rather a hurry this evening. I have a hairdressing appointment, and I must get to a community meeting afterwards. Unfortunately, my car is in a garage being serviced, so I must bus back and forth, but I wanted to grab a couple of books for Mother."

Sheila gestured towards the crime novel section of the bookshelves.

"I know that she likes Agatha Christie stories, Miss Stanley, though I think that she has read most of them. Perhaps she would enjoy a mystery novel by Perry Mason?"

Jean shook her head.

"No, I do not think so. He is an American author, isn't he? I took her a book by Raymond Chandler once, and she was horrified by the dialogue. She is quite old-fashioned but also getting very forgetful, so even though she may have read an Agatha Christie book, she may not remember."

Ten Little Indians and *The Murder of Roger Ackroyd* were selected and taken to the counter to be stamped.

As Jean produced her mother's library card, she commented, "I do not understand my mother's interest in crime stories, but they seem to be her literary taste these days. Thanks, Sheila, I must dash."

She pushed the two books into an already overfull satchel and made her way to the door. She paused as the receptionist called out, "Is the meeting about the annual dance, Miss Stanley? I always enjoy going to that. Will it be the same band as last year?"

"Possibly, Sheila, but I do not know for sure. It has not yet been arranged. Bye."

The rain had eased as Jean exited the library, though the pavement was slippery underfoot, and the gutter was a swollen river. She glanced at her watch. No time now for her usual shampoo and set. She would have to make do with a crop and a tidy-up. She almost ran the hundred yards to the salon with the satchel clasped to her chest. Thankfully, just a few customers were inside and a vacant seat awaited.

"No time for my usual, Marion. Just a quick bob and tidy-up, please."

The stylist placed a covering apron over Jean's shoulders and produced scissors and a comb. Her hand ran through Jean's hair which had been darkened by the rain from its usual natural honey-blonde colouring.

"It is a shame that you feel the need to crop your hair at all, Miss Stanley. If I had your hair, I would let it grow all down my back."

Jean noted the envious tone with appreciation but remarked, "I am a schoolteacher. I need to look practical and efficient rather than glamorous but thank you for the compliment."

With the crop completed with Jean's impatient urging, the stylist removed the gown, picked up the satchel from beside the chair and handed it over. Jean paid for the crop with an additional tip, checked her watch again and hurriedly exited the salon. Too hurriedly, for she ran straight into the path of a military-style raincoated male who was passing by. She almost stumbled and reached out a hand to avoid falling over. The satchel slipped from her grasp. It was prevented from falling to the pavement by a strong arm that reached out and grabbed it. Embarrassedly, Jean looked up into the face of the man who had held it. He smiled at her hasty apology.

"It is not often that I get almost knocked off my feet by a young lady! Are you alright?"

Jean nodded. "I am so sorry. I was in a hurry to catch a bus."

The man nodded and handed her the satchel.

"More haste, less speed, as they say. Are you sure that you are not hurt?"

"I am fine, thank you," Jean replied to the shadowy figure.

"Then I will be on my way. I hope that you catch your bus."

Another smile beamed down on Jean before the man strode purposefully away. Almost reluctantly, she watched him go, temporarily forgetting about the bus she was desperate to catch. She walked up to the traffic lights at the intersection and waited anxiously for the lights to turn green. It was with a sense of horror that she saw the Bucton single-decker approach the lights from the opposite direction. The bus stop was in the market square a hundred yards away on the opposite side of the road. Missing the bus meant another hour's wait for the next one, by which time the association meeting would have begun. Jean sensed the annoyance of the chairwoman, Lady Raeburn, if she was not there to take the minutes.

Taking her life in her hands, she attempted to sprint across the road as soon as the lights changed to amber. She almost made it. Two-thirds of the way across, she slipped on a patch of motor oil and sprawled headlong. The satchel hit the ground hard and slithered over the wet tarmac to land against the opposite kerb. The flap burst open and spilled part of its contents on the edge of the road. Jean lay still, feeling pain in her elbows and knees until she realised that traffic was swerving around her. She struggled to her feet and limped to the pavement, where she sat on the edge of the kerb for a minute or so before bending down to retrieve the broken satchel and the exercise books and other items which had spilled out. She uttered a word that her mother often used in annoyance.

"Feathers," she exclaimed as her right ankle sent a message to her brain that it was also damaged. "Obviously, this is not my lucky day."

The Bucton bus, now drawing away from the market square with the driver oblivious to her plight, gave emphasis to her comment. Not for the first time, Jean realised how isolated her village was from the mainstream of life. Only occasionally would a vehicle turn off to take the road to it. Little happened there that was of great import; the resident population had hardly grown over the years, and most lived insular lives within the local community, being employed at the quarry business owned by Sir Joshua Raeburn.

Jean's father, Henry Stanley, had also spent his life working at the quarry and only taken semi-retirement when diagnosed with a tumour in his lung. Jean remembered him telling her after the surgery that removed the carcinoma that he needed to keep working. He did not have any hobbies to occupy his mind, and the thought of all the empty hours sitting idly at home filled him with dread. His happy relationship with his wife had declined because of her melancholia caused by the death of their three-month-old son, Simon, from meningitis. No psychiatric treatment had been beneficial in lifting the gloom of their loss; the strong bond between husband and wife had vanished overnight. Henry had also been deeply upset by the premature death of his young son, but his wife seemed to have no understanding of that.

Jean had been at university when Simon was born and was never able to establish a bond with the baby during his short life. She shared the grief and sense of loss of her parents but was more disturbed by her mother's state of mind and the broken bond with her father. It saddened her to see her father distressed and isolated in the family home. It was the reason that she had taken the teaching post at the local primary school. Both parents required mental support, and she needed to be at home to provide it. Her father's illness had strengthened that belief, though he had recovered well from the lung surgery.

She did not approve of him going back to work at the quarry but understood his motive for doing so. It was an escape from his wife's brooding silences. Henry had implored Sir Joshua to keep him on part-time, and his employer, with respect for a man who had given him long and faithful service, had acceded to that request with a sedentary position in a small wooden building perched high up on the edge of the quarry that served as an office and an observation post. Here, Jean's father could look down on the workforce and direct operations while remaining unexposed to the dust which rose and swirled around the quarry floor. Jean had visited him there on one or two occasions and had been disturbed by the precarious position of the hut and its timber sides, which were slightly askew due to the constant buffeting from the wind. Her parent had assured her that he was perfectly safe, and the hut provided a perfect viewpoint into the depths of the quarry. Jean could do no more than kiss his cheek and tell him not to take any risks.

Chapter 3

Sitting on the edge of the stone kerb, Jean became aware of the chill that was spreading through her body. She shivered and realised that she had to move despite the pain in her ankle. She glanced behind at the wooden seat beside the bus stop. She needed to get to it to wait for the next bus. Jean slowly picked up the satchel and got to her feet; she realised that her umbrella had been left behind at the library or during the run to the hairdressing salon. It did not matter. She was already drenched through. Her tights were in tatters, and her dress was clinging wetly to her thighs under her coat. With limping steps, wincing every time she put a leg forward, she reached the bench and thankfully sat down. It was a full five minutes before she took stock of herself. A seeping graze on her exposed left knee showed bloody evidence of her fall; her right elbow felt tight and painful. She ran her hand through her wet, cropped hair with a sigh of dismay, thankful she had not opted for the more costly coiffeur.

She turned her attention to the satchel and checked that the two library books were safe and dry inside. Several of the school exercise books that had tipped out onto the road were not in such good condition. Some had torn pages, while others had illegible writing where the wet ink had run.

"Feathers," Jean exclaimed again. She would have a job marking these pages and eventually must apologise to the authors.

Jean was still delving through the satchel when a silver soft-topped Bentley sports model motor car drove into the market square and stopped in front of the bench. Jean looked up startled as the driver wound down a window. Through the gloom, she recognised the face of the male she had encountered an hour or so previously.

"Hullo again! When we bumped into each other outside the hairdressing salon, I had the feeling that we were destined to meet again, though not so quickly or in such uncomfortable circumstances. I saw your tumble when I came out of my father's office. I realised it was you when I saw the satchel slither across the road, but it took me a few minutes to pick up my car and drive over here. Can I be of any help? I noticed that the bus you were going to catch has left. I have nothing of importance to do this evening, so I can take you where you wish to go."

Jean felt her cheeks reddening and her body tremble, though neither was the result of the wet and cold. She managed to stammer, "Thank you. You are very kind, but I can wait for the next bus. I will be fine once I get home."

The slight quiver in her voice was heard but misinterpreted. The driver's door opened; four quick strides took the tall, athletic figure to her side. He gazed down at her.

"Oh, Lord! You are in a sorry state! You cannot sit here in that condition. Please allow me to help you. I notice that you have some bumps and bruises from your fall. Can you stand up alright?"

Jean hesitated while looking up at the handsome face. He seemed to be genuinely concerned, but could he be trusted? She had often warned her female pupils not to accept lifts from strangers. She decided to err on the side of caution.

"I am OK, I think, apart from spraining my ankle. Just wet, really. I can wait here for the next bus."

The response was emphatic, accompanied by a quick shake of the head.

"No, no. You will catch pneumonia. Besides, a true gentleman never leaves a damsel in distress. Where do you live? You were waiting for the bus to Bucton, were you not? That is not far. I can have you home in a jiffy. You need to get out of those wet clothes and have a hot soak in the bath."

He smiled down at Jean.

"If you have sprained your ankle, which it appears that you have, I can help you to my car and you can rest it on the back seat."

Dazzled by his smile and not looking forward to waiting another hour for the next bus, Jean threw caution to the winds.

"Very well. Thank you."

A supporting arm was held out as she rose to her feet, trying not to put any weight on her injured foot. She became acutely conscious of the arm that suddenly encircled her waist and lifted her left side so that her leg was clear of the ground. The movement drew Jean closer to a muscular shoulder, and she caught the faint scent of aftershave as she was half-carried to the Bentley. Gently propped up against the left wing, Jean waited while the passenger door was opened and kept wide. She struggled into the back seat with as much dignity as she could muster, aware that every movement was being watched as she swung her legs around.

"Well done! Just relax while I pick up your satchel."

Jean watched her rescuer walk back to the bench, scoop up the broken school bag and return. There was no doubt about his charm and attractiveness: the intimacy of the closeness of their contact as with each limping step their hips touched and broke apart on the way to the Bentley had caused a quickening of her heartbeat. At the same time, she felt rather disturbed by his self-confidence. It hinted that he was a man who was used to getting his own way. Not that his facets of character were any concern of hers. Once he had taken her home, he would wish her luck and go on his way. She would remember him as a good Samaritan; he, if he thought of her at all, would recall her as a muddy dishevelled girl to whom he had given a lift, and that would be the end of it.

The satchel was placed on the seat beside Jean.

"Right, soon have you home now. Can you manage your seatbelt?"

An arm was extended towards the seatbelt, but Jean grabbed the hanging strap before a move was made to pass it over her body and guide it into its retainer. Watchful eyes followed her movement as she secured herself. A nod of approval came before the driver strode round to settle himself in the front driving seat. He flashed a smile back at Jean before switching on the engine and disengaging the hand brake.

"Tallyho, then. Off we go!"

Chapter 4

With the Bentley purring along the Bucton Road and her rescuer concentrating on the road, Jean was able to take stock of him more closely, courtesy of the driving mirror. He had certainly taken control of the situation, and she could not fault his considerate behaviour, but he was still a stranger, and she was unsure of his motive in offering assistance. Neither of them had introduced themselves: perhaps it was because so much had happened in a short space of time. Perhaps it was because the man did not want to identify himself for personal reasons. Jean shifted nervously in her seat and had a moment of panic. Supposing his charm was a facade, and he was luring her to a desolate spot on Bucton Tor where she would be subjected to sexual abuse or murdered? She looked at the back of the driver's head and, for a moment, saw him transformed into Arthur Conan Doyle's Mr Hyde.

Jean peered sideways through the window beside her and tried to gauge the speed of the car. If she opened the back door and jumped out, would the force of the impact on the road cause serious injury or death? Could she pick herself up and run away? She instantly realised that she could not. Her ankle injury plus the painful graze on her right knee would not allow her to get very far. She was at the mercy of the man in front of her. She wished that she'd listened to her own warnings to her pupils. Her hand moved to the door handle. Mr Hyde saw the movement out of the corner of his eye and looked back at her.

"Are you alright?" he asked. "You are not going to pass out on me, are you? Do you want me to stop for a moment?"

The look of concern on his face allayed Jean's fears. How could she be so silly? In the classroom she always had control.

This moment of alarm was so unlike her. Jekyll's evil alter ego vanished from her imagination. She eased back in her seat, the terror clearing her mind. When she spoke, her voice was quite calm.

"No, I felt a little queasy for a moment, but I am alright now. Perhaps I could have my window opened just a little?"

"Of course!"

The window was slid down an inch or two as a button was pressed.

"How's that? Do you smoke? Would you like a cigarette?"

"No, I don't, but thanks."

Jean had stopped trembling, but she had given herself a headache, and her injured ankle was beginning to throb.

Her companion glanced at her.

"I think that I should stop for a moment. You do look rather pale. It is still raining, but if I wind the window right down you can get some air."

The car was brought to a halt and the window fully opened. It was pitch black outside the perimeter of the headlights. There were no overhead lamps or cats' eyes in the road. The few houses situated on the hillside were so distant that their illuminated interiors flickered hazily in the rain like dying fireflies. Only the rain pelting on the Bentley's soft rooftop disturbed the silence. Both the car's occupants stared out for a few moments before the driver turned to Jean.

Apologetically he remarked, "Do you realise that I do not know your name? Here I am, taking a distressed young lady home, and I do not know what to call you?"

He smiled at Jean. "My name is Mark, by the way!"

Jean held out a hand and returned his smile.

"I am sorry. I should have also introduced myself. My name is Jean. Jean Stanley."

Mark nodded, showing even white teeth that Jean presumed would be in the care of a private dentist.

"A pleasure to meet you, Jean, though I wish the circumstances were different. Forgive me, but I could not help noticing the school exercise books in your satchel. Are you a teacher?"

"I teach English at the local primary, plus other subjects when required!"

"Such as?"

"Art. PE. Drama occasionally."

"A noble profession, school teaching, I've always thought. Lucky Jones minor, or are you a dragon under that lovely exterior – a sugar-coated pill, so to speak? No, no, of course not."

Mark's searching eyes travelled swiftly over her upper frame. In a regretful tone, he said, "Too bad I did not have you to teach me my Latin verse instead of Montague-Smyth."

Jean laughed. "I doubt if I would have had much success. If you will forgive me, you do not seem the studious type to me."

The grin returned.

"You are quite right. I am not. Swotting dry dusty tomes held no interest for me. What use is there for Latin, except for writing medical prescriptions that nobody can read anyway? Why learn history when it is the present that counts? I can speak the Queen's English; I know the biology of the human species. Experience is the best teacher, and I am quite content to be its pupil."

"Experience often has a cane in its hand," was Jean's dry comment.

Mark chuckled.

"Touché. I have a feeling that you and I will get along famously. Anyway, it sounds as if you keep yourself busy! What do you do in any leisure time?"

"Not very much, I'm afraid. I am on the local social and entertainment committee at Bucton and was due to attend a meeting this evening. The annual dance at the village hall will be taking place next month, and there is much to discuss. I am not sure if I will make it now."

Mark nodded his agreement.

"It looks unlikely with that ankle needing attention. My advice is to forget about the meeting, have a hot soak in a tub and then make yourself comfortable on a sofa. You can telephone your apologies. Someone should be able to step into your shoes just for tonight."

Jean shook her head.

"I do not think that the chairwoman, Lady Raeburn, would take kindly to my absence. She always expects me to take the minutes."

To Jean's astonishment, Mark threw his back and let out a roar of laughter.

"Good Lord, Jean, that dear lady is my aunt! I know what an old dragon Beatrice can be at times, but I think that she is fond of me. When I explain what has happened that is preventing you from getting to the meeting, she will understand. Do not concern yourself! I can relay your apologies. Now, let me get you home."

Mark wound up the window, let out the clutch and pressed the accelerator. The Bentley roared and leapt forward into the rain-filled darkness, with Jean staring with astonishment at the back of Mark's head.

Chapter 5

With the car speeding along towards Bucton and Mark concentrating on driving, Jean scrutinised his features more closely in order to find some similarity with the familiar countenance of Lady Raeburn. She could find none. Were they really related? His comment proved that he was aware of her strong character, but the chairwoman had never mentioned having a nephew. Jean suddenly realised that if that was indeed true, then the man driving her home had to be the son of her father's employer, Sir Joshua Raeburn.

Jean rarely listened to village gossip, but she could not avoid hearing all the talk among the residents about Mark Raeburn's lifestyle. She remembered the stories that had circulated regarding Mark's various amours, little titbits of scandal that the gossipers had whispered and gloried in. The local community of Bucton was closely bound up with the affairs of the Raeburn family since most of the village menfolk were either employed at the quarry or the Punting cement works, both of which were owned and controlled by Mark's father.

Sir John had always taken an active interest in the affairs of his employees and their families, but his son had shown no such concern. While his father presided over committee meetings and attended various village functions and sports events, Mark was engaged in a social whirl with Punting's upper set. These 'immoral pursuits' condemned him in the eyes of the simple, hardworking mining folk, but their main prejudice was caused by his lack of interest in his father's business activities. They felt that he should have shouldered some of Sir John's burden of responsibilities, whereas it was apparent that the mining industry held no attraction for him.

In due course, he would succeed to the management of the family businesses, but in the meantime he was happy to engage in idle pursuits.

Jean studied Mark's profile again. His jawline was firm and strong; his hands on the wheel were well-manicured and capable. He looked utterly dependable, and yet there was a hint of recklessness about his whole bearing that lent confirmation to his reputation for irresponsibility. Whatever his reputation, Jean could find no fault with his behaviour towards her since they had first bumped into each other outside the hairdressing salon. He had been courteous and kind, and she had been rather bewitched by his charm, but was he only a ladies' man with little strength of character? Jean was determined to find out. She was deep in thought when she saw the lights of Bucton ahead.

"We are almost there now, Mark. Please turn left at the bottom of the hill."

Five minutes later, the car stopped outside the grey stone cottage that nestled close in the lee of the hill; the yellow honeysuckle on the fence beside the front gate wafted its fragrance to the car's two occupants. For a moment they sat still, inhaling the sweet scent and enjoying the quietness of the evening as the engine was switched off.

Mark turned to Jean.

"Stay where you are. You cannot walk on that ankle. I will come round your side and help you out. Will your parents be at home?"

Jean nodded. "Mother will be. I can manage to hop to the door."

Mark looked at her with a frown on his forehead but a quizzical smile on his lips.

"Hop? Do you seriously believe that I would allow you to hop up the garden path on one leg? Nonsense, my dear girl! I am going to carry you to the door, and please, no argument about it. I am coming around to your side to open the door. I want you to swing your legs around and face me, and then put your arms around my neck as I bend forward. Do you think that you can manage that?"

Jean could feel herself blushing. She hesitated, then nodded. In an instant Mark was beside her, opening the door.

"Right, slide towards me as far as you can and then swing your legs around."

Jean did as she was instructed while wishing she had worn a fuller length skirt and worried that the garment she was wearing was clinging wetly to her thighs. Mark appeared not to notice.

"Come on. Put your arms around my neck."

In one effortless movement, he scooped Jean up. She found her neck cradled into his and caught another whiff of masculine perfume. She closed her eyes, conscious of one strong arm under her knees and the other around her waist.

"Well done," she heard Mark say. "Do you have a key?"

Jean searched her coat pocket with a free hand but could not find it.

"Never mind. I will knock."

As Mark carried her up the garden path, Jean imagined herself as a bride about to be carried across the threshold and felt herself blushing again. Then sanity returned and she tensed in his arms. Her rescuer mistook her movement.

"I will not drop you, so do not worry. Keep your arms around my neck as I knock. I will go and collect your satchel from the car as soon as you are safely inside."

Slow footsteps were heard inside before the door was cautiously opened, and the slim figure of Jean's mother peered out. Her eyes widened, and one hand flew to her mouth as she gasped at seeing her daughter in the arms of a man who she thought she recognised.

"*Jean!* What has happened?"

"I am all right, Mother. It's just a twisted ankle. I had a fall in town. This gentleman has been kind enough to drive me home."

Mrs Stanley opened the door wide to enable Jean to be carried into the living room, where she was gently deposited on the nearest armchair. Mark turned to face Jean's mother and extended his hand.

"My name is Mark Raeburn, Mrs Stanley. It's a pleasure to meet you."

Ann Stanley had recovered some composure on hearing her daughter's calm statement, but her spine seemed to stiffen as he confirmed his identity. She gazed at Mark and answered politely.

"Thank you, Mr Raeburn. It was kind of you to bring my daughter home. May I offer you tea or coffee?"

Mark smiled.

"Thank you, but no. I have another engagement that l must attend to, but I hope you will allow me to check on your daughter in a day or two. I am sure that she will be fine after a hot bath and some attention to the ankle and the other bruising she sustained when tripping over in town. Please excuse me while I collect her satchel from my car."

He smiled and left, returning quickly with the open satchel and placing it on a nearby small table.

"I am afraid some of the contents are quite wet when they were spilled out onto the road, but I hope that they are salvageable."

He bent over Jean and placed a firm hand on her coat sleeve. She glanced up at him.

"Thank you. You have been very kind. Without your help, I would have probably lost most of them."

Mark shook his head while keeping his eyes fixed on Jean.

"Glad to be of service. I hope that we can meet again under more pleasurable circumstances."

He turned to Mrs Stanley, who was standing quietly behind him, observing his every move.

"I suggest that your daughter gets out of those wet clothes as soon as possible, otherwise she will be sneezing her head off tomorrow!"

Mrs Stanley nodded.

"I will see to it, Mr Raeburn. Allow me to see you out first."

Mark was escorted to the door, which was closed firmly after he had walked up the garden path.

Ann Stanley returned to her daughter and looked down almost accusingly.

"You do know who he is, don't you?"

"Yes, of course, Mother. He is Lady Raeburn's nephew."

"Did he also tell you that he is a womaniser and a wastrel who has never done a job in his life?"

Jean shifted uncomfortably in the armchair.

"No, Mother, he did not, but he was very kind and considerate, and I owe him a debt of gratitude. I will have my bath now if you can help me upstairs."

Later that evening, with her injured ankle strapped up and soothing lotion applied to her bruises after the hot bath, Jean lay in her bed and pondered on the day's events. Her pulse quickened when she remembered the close contact with Mark and the masculinity of his strong arms around her when he lifted her out of the car. Her last memory before she drifted off to sleep was the keenness of his gaze from the bluest of eyes that held the depth of an ocean.

Chapter 6

Jean woke up early the next morning and checked her damaged ankle. Her grazed knee had been bandaged, but she felt a twinge of pain as she stood up and went downstairs to the kitchen. It was fortunate that she did not have to go back to school until the beginning of the next term. She wondered if the entertainments committee the previous evening had made any decisions about the annual dance and, more importantly, if Mark had passed on the reason for Jean's absence. She hoped so, for the last thing she wanted was to get a telephone call from the chairwoman voicing her displeasure that Jean had not been available to take the minutes.

Jean made a cup of coffee and sat in the kitchen to drink it. It was all quiet in the house, so it was likely that her mother would still be in bed. There was no evidence of unwashed crockery in the sink to suggest that her father had breakfasted and gone to the quarry. Probably he was still asleep in the separate bedroom he had occupied since his wife had isolated herself. Jean had sat with him for a while after having her bath and had told him about her fall in Punting and the subsequent rescue by Mark Raeburn. With her mother closeted in her bedroom with the new novels, Jean had been able to ask her father what he knew about Mark's dubious reputation.

Henry Stanley was not a man who took notice of rumours, preferring to form his own opinion of a person and make a sober judgement of their character based on facts. The many accounts of Mark's cavalier lifestyle had reached his ears so often that it had to be conceded that there had to be an element of truth in them. On hearing his daughter's story of Mark's assistance following her mishap, he contented himself by acknowledging the chivalrous conduct of his employer's son, though he was cynical enough to believe that Mark's gentlemanly behaviour could have been a ploy to gain favour in the eyes of a very attractive girl. Knowing his daughter's strength of will and the high standards she expected of herself and those with whom she was acquainted, Henry was confident that she would not be easily fooled by handsome looks or superficial charm. If she had entertained any thought of having a friendly relationship with Mark, he would have to prove himself worthy of it.

Chapter 7

The call from Mark two days later caught Jean completely by surprise. Her heart leaped in her chest as she heard the deep tone of his voice.

"Hi, it's me."

He was confident enough not to identify himself.

Jean momentarily hesitated, her mother's rather virulent condemnation of the caller at the back of her mind. She decided to play it cool.

"Oh, hullo. Is it Mr Raeburn? How kind of you to call."

"It's Mark, remember? How is your ankle? Strong enough for you to come and have some lunch with me?"

Jean tried to stop her excitement from mounting. Her reply was contained.

"It is fine now, thank you. I am afraid that I cannot accept your invitation, though. I have several things to do today, including picking up my car from the repair garage."

"Oh." The disappointment in Mark's voice was obvious.

"Are you sure? I am well known in most of the restaurants and have no need to book."

"I have no doubt about that, Mark, but I really cannot make it today."

"Oh."

Jean detected a tone that was not used to rejection.

"Well, how about tomorrow, then. I can pick you up about 1pm?"

Jean laughed at his persistence, but she really did want to see him again.

"Well, alright, then, but just for lunch. I will be ready at one o'clock."

The voice brightened. "Good girl! One o'clock on the dot, then."

Jean replaced the receiver. She had never approved of deception of any kind, but she thought that it would be prudent not to inform her mother of the lunch date; in view of her parents' low opinion of Lady Raeburn's nephew, there would be some disapproval. Her father would be less obdurate but would still advise some caution about the possible development of a relationship which may end up with his daughter being emotionally hurt.

Chapter 8

Sitting opposite Mark at the restaurant dining table, Jean felt a fluttering of her heart. There was no doubt that he was an attractive man, and she felt quite strongly drawn to him. She tried to push her emotions aside. This was just a lunch after all, and accepting his invitation was no more than a grateful response for the help her dining companion had provided. Nevertheless, she felt her cheeks burning at his intense gaze and turned her head away to look around the room.

"This is very nice. Do you come here often, Mark?"

Mark looked amused.

"It is one of my haunts. The food is usually good. I hope you will like it."

A wine waiter was hovering expectantly. Mark beckoned him closer before asking Jean, "Do you want to see the wine list, or shall I choose? Do you prefer red or white? They have an excellent cellar here."

Jean smiled but shook her head.

"Thank you, but no. I rarely drink alcohol at this time of day."

The thought of drinking wine when she already felt intoxicated by the intensity of Mark's eyes caused her some alarm. She needed to clear her head, not add more instability to it.

Reluctantly, Mark waved the waiter away.

"Soup, then? They serve an excellent chicken and mushroom consommé."

Jean relaxed.

"Thank you. That sounds very nice. I am sure that I will enjoy that."

Mark proved an interesting conversationalist throughout the meal that followed and recited many anecdotes that kept Jean amused. She was grateful that he did not try to flirt with her or ask her questions about her private life, and she was sorry when coffee finally arrived to end the lunch.

As Mark walked Jean back to her car, he made a move to bend over to kiss her on the cheek, but she took a step backwards and held out her hand.

"Thank you, Mark. I enjoyed the meal and your company. And thank you for telling your aunt the reason I could not get to the committee meeting. It saved me an awkward phone call."

Mark smiled.

"No problem, Jean. I hope the annual dance goes well."

He watched her drive away before walking over to his own vehicle.

Chapter 9

During the next few weeks, Mark called Jean several times to invite her for an evening out for a meal or to visit a theatre. She had thought about him quite often since the pub lunch, but always at the back of her mind was his reputation for philandering. She did not want to be another notch on his bedpost.

Apart from Ben, she had not had many boyfriends even in her college days because she was so concentrated on her teaching career and had rarely dated. She enjoyed male company but had not met anyone who had stirred her interest. Except Mark. He had disturbed her emotions and her mind far more than she had previously experienced, but she was level-headed enough to realise the danger those feelings evoked. She could not allow herself to fall in love with a man who looked on life as a playground without any work ethic.

Mark Raeburn was the son and heir of the aristocratic quarry owner and had no need to work with the large financial allowance his father gave him, but should he not have a sense of duty in helping his father with his businesses and earn his income through his own industrious efforts? Her own father had worked all his life for everything he owned and had even scraped together the money to send Jean to university. His reward for that achievement was his sense of pride and the happiness of his daughter in giving her the opportunity to make her dream come true.

Mark would never have an awareness of self-respect while he indulged in his frivolous lifestyle. In order to make himself worthy of Jean's love, he had to prove himself capable of behaving more diligently and industriously. Besides which, of course, Jean was not looking for an early marriage because she was so devoted to her teaching career. She had even turned down Ben's proposal of marriage, though the reason was that her fondness for him had not escalated into any more than deep friendship.

Chapter 10

On the evening of the annual social dance, Jean arrived at the community hall quite early to ensure that everything had been done to make the evening a success. Local volunteers had festooned the hall with brightly coloured ribbons and glowing lights: a large wooden dais had been erected at one end for the five-piece band, who were busy setting up their instruments and rehearsing their repertoire of chosen music. At the other end of the room, a long table held a vast repast of savouries under its snowy white covering, courtesy of local housewives well known for their cooking skills.

A small adjoining room became the bar area where a variety of drinks could be obtained. The manager of the public house that had supplied the liquid refreshment had given his assurance to Lady Raeburn that a responsible bartender would limit the consumption of alcohol. In turn, she had reminded him with a steely look that licensing laws needed to be obeyed and underage youngsters should be served non-alcoholic drinks only. She stood by the main entrance to the hall as partygoers arrived to ensure that no young males would be admitted if they looked inebriated. Both she and Jean failed to notice the arrival of Ben, who had slipped in quietly behind another young couple and positioned himself in a corner of the hall where he could observe Jean as she moved around the room.

Gradually the hall began to fill up and the band began to perform welcoming music. One middle-aged couple took the floor and began to dance. Other couples followed. The female vocalist came on stage and rendered a popular version of the latest hit tune. Music, laughter and the hubbub of conversations filled the air. Jean accepted the invitation to dance from a local young man whose family she had known for many years. She turned away when the dance ended but then felt a tap on her shoulder. She expected to see the young man requesting another dance but instead found herself looking into Mark's smiling face. He extended a hand.

"May I have the honour of the next dance, mademoiselle?" he asked.

Taken completely by surprise, Jean hesitated before exclaiming, "Mark! What are you doing here?"

"I am afraid that I have gate-crashed, but since I knew that you would be here, I could not resist coming along."

The right hand stayed extended. Jean smiled and placed her own hand in his.

"It's nice to see you, Mark."

She moved closer and placed her other hand on his shoulder as the band began to play a slow waltz. In the corner of the room, Ben took a step forward and clenched his fists. His face turned to a scowl as Mark manoeuvred Jean around the dance floor and held on to her as the waltz ended.

"I have booked you as my dance partner for the rest of the evening." Mark smiled down at her. "I hope you do not mind?"

Jean glanced up into his handsome face but shook her head in apology.

"Sorry, Mark. Your aunt has charged me to keep circulating in order to check that everyone here is happy and enjoying themselves. Perhaps later? Why don't you go into the bar and get yourself a drink? I will join you when I am free."

Mark reluctantly released her hand.

"Is that a promise?"

Jean nodded and gave him a gentle push.

"Yes, now go!"

She watched him walk towards the bar room and turned away to chat to a young couple close by. She did not see Ben closely follow Mark into the outer drinks area. It was fifteen minutes later when she was at the other end of the hall that she was told of an altercation between two males at the drinks bar. Hurriedly, she went to investigate. She found Mark confronted by a red-faced, very angry Ben, who she had not noticed previously.

She heard him shout, "She is too good for you! Why don't you go and find someone else to flirt with? You don't belong here, anyway! You have never shown any interest in local community affairs before!"

Mark looked down at Ben from his 6ft 3in height and pushed away the flailing fist that threatened him.

He said amusedly, "It's none of your business with whom I choose to associate. You have had too much to drink. I suggest you go before you get into trouble."

Jean stepped forward to come between them before an outraged Ben made another lunge forward. She held out a restraining hand and said firmly, "Please, Ben, this is not the time or place to have a personal disagreement. You are a dear friend, but I think you need to calm down. Just go home, and I will talk to you tomorrow."

She bent forward to place a kiss on his cheek and then beckoned to a security guard to escort Ben to the exit door.

Mark was standing still, rather taken aback by Jean's affectionate gesture. She touched him gently on the arm.

"Mark, I need to talk to you, but I do not have time right now. There will be an interval in about half an hour when the band will have a rest and the food table will be uncovered. I will meet you there."

Jean returned to the main hall, but her mind remained at the bar area, replaying the scene she had witnessed and remembering Ben's angry outburst. She knew that there was some justification for the accusations hurled at Mark. If there was to be a future relationship with Sir Joshua's son, he had to learn that he needed to think seriously about his future and of her own ambition to continue her teaching career. However much she was attracted to him – and she still felt the thrill of his embrace when they were dancing – nothing would change those intentions.

Chapter 11

Mark was desultorily turning over a vol-au-vent in his hands when she found him three-quarters of an hour later. He put it back on the table as Jean approached. She faced him squarely.

"We need to talk privately. May we go and sit in your car?"

Mark nodded and led the way to where his Bentley was parked. Sitting side by side in the front seats, they turned to each other.

Jean placed her hands in her lap and quietly said, "Mark, there are things that you need to understand. Ben Haywood, the man who confronted you at the bar, is a lifelong friend of mine. We grew up together when we were little children and, in fact, were constant companions until we were teenagers and I went off to teaching college. I am very fond of him, but he developed deeper feelings for me and asked me to marry him. I turned him down because I wanted to pursue my ambition to become a teacher and, frankly, because I was unsure whether he would be the ideal husband for me. He can be rather irresponsible, and I need a man who I can rely on and will always support me. Apart from that, both my parents are ageing, and neither of them are in very good health, mentally or physically. I am their only child since they lost my baby brother, and I cannot leave them to get married while they need me. It is the reason I took the vacant teaching post at the local primary school so that I am available to help them whenever necessary. I explained all that to Ben, but he finds it hard to accept that I will never be anything but a good friend. I will always be here for him, but I will never be his wife. The problem is that he is jealous of any other man that takes an interest in me, so, Mark, you need to be aware of that and avoid contact with him. Not that you are likely to, since you mix in completely different social circles. In any event, although he can be impetuous, I have never known him to act violently. This incident at the bar really surprised me."

Mark had listened in silence, but as she finished, he leaned forward, placed a hand over her two clasped hands and responded.

"Thank you for explaining your relationship, Jean. Now I understand his irate behaviour. I have only known you for a short while, but I was also attracted to you from almost the first glance. You are different from many of the other women I have known; you are intelligent, obviously very caring and with the courage to follow your dream despite all the hurdles you may need to overcome. I would not be here this evening if I did not want to know more about you. I have asked you on more than one occasion if you would allow me to escort you to a social event if you were not engaged, but you have turned down my invitations. It may be that among the local mining community, I do not have a creditable reputation. Your young man was right that I have not shown much interest in local affairs, and perhaps I should have offered more assistance to my father in his business dealings. I realise that he must have expected me to take over the management of the quarry at some time in the future and will be disappointed that I have not involved myself in local matters in preparation for his retirement. Frankly, Jean, it is not how I want to spend the rest of my life. I have been cast in a different mould from my father. An experience at university proved to me that life can be short, and you should enjoy all the pleasure and excitement that you can find while you are young. One of my classmates was very studious and spent all his time swotting for the grades he needed in order to fulfil his dream of being a research scientist in tropical diseases. He had a brilliant mind and would have achieved his ambition if he had not been killed in a freak accident when a tree that was struck by lightning during a storm fell on top of his car and crushed him to death."

Jean nodded sympathetically.

"Mark, that is a very sad story, but we all know how uncertain life can be. Your friend was unlucky to be in the wrong place at the wrong time. You cannot allow that one unfortunate circumstance to affect the rest of your life. In memory of your friend, you need to attempt to contribute to society in a way that would please him. That will help to improve the lives of others; you may not gain the excitement you crave, but you will gain your reward from the respect of the community. I suggest that you approach your father and offer him your active support. I am sure he will be very pleased to hear it."

She paused for a moment and glanced at her watch.

"Talking of Sir John, I think that we should get back to the hall. He is expected to arrive and hand out awards to those members of his workforce who have contributed to the improved sales of the mining quarry this past year. No doubt your aunt will also be looking for me."

Chapter 12

Two days after the annual dance event, Jean encountered Ben in the village while she was shopping. She reproached him for his angry outburst at Mark and told him that Sir Joshua's son was just a friend and someone who had helped her when she had a fall in town. She had met him only once since then for lunch, so there was no need for Ben to be jealous. She had been made aware of Mark's reputation and had no intention of becoming seriously involved with him. Her ambitions remained unchanged; her teaching career was her priority.

Ben was unconvinced but told her that he had returned to live with his parents and had been given his crane driver job back at the quarry. Jean was pleased to hear that news and suggested that he found a girlfriend with whom he might form a relationship. Ben shook his head and walked away, seemingly not hearing Jean's last pleading comment: 'Try to stay out of trouble!'

A day after this encounter with Ben, Jean had a conversation with her father about Mark, who had rung her to ask if he could take her out again. Henry told her he had no serious objections. She was old enough to make her own decisions, but he reminded her of Mark's loose reputation.

"Jean, you are wise enough not to listen to gossip, but I suggest that you take your time to get to know Mark better before you form a serious relationship. I want you to find the right man to fall in love with and who will be fully committed to you and make you happy. I know that you have dedicated yourself to a teaching career, but I am old-fashioned enough to want to see you happily married and hopefully provide me with a grandson. I lost your young brother, and your mother and I no longer have the same loving bond because of his death. A young child running around the house may bring back sad memories, but ultimately it may bring us closer together again.

Jean leaned forward and gave her father an affectionate hug. She said gently, "Dad, one day I will get married and hopefully give you the grandchild you want, but right now, my teaching comes first. I took the post at the local primary school specifically so that I could live here with you and Mother and care for you when necessary. And do not worry about Mark. I am attracted to him, but I am concerned about his irresponsible reputation. He has to prove that he is worthy of my love."

Jean smoothed the few remaining white hairs on her father's head, took hold of one of his gnarled hands, noting the brown kidney spots on the back, and looked at him reassuringly.

"Don't worry about me, Dad. I am a big girl now, and I have your sense of responsibility to guide me."

Henry Stanley looked at his daughter with a softened expression and a look of bright affection in his eyes.

"To be honest, Jean, I do not know what I would have done without you during the last few years. Your mother seldom talks to me now. I worry about her, but I cannot seem to help her."

Jean bent over and kissed his furrowed brow. Softly she said, "With some love and care, Dad, we will restore that special bond between you. Until then, I am not going anywhere."

Jean returned to her primary school at the beginning of the new term. There were a few fresh faces in her class, and she greeted them with her usual warmth and good humour. She loved this group of students and their untrained minds. Teaching them was like planting a garden in uncultivated soil. First, it had to be fertilised and enriched with kindness and understanding before the seeds of knowledge could be planted. In whose minds would plants succeed or wither and die? Whose minds would need more feeding and receive extra attention so the seeds would thrive and grow strong? Which part of the garden is the best situation for some plants? In full sun or shade, where do they feel more comfortable? Jean had to assess the character of all the young individuals and determine which of her seedlings would become hardy perennial plants or tender annuals. She would only know that through each lesson and at the end of term. Jean felt that she had an important role to play in training young minds and helping to develop character. Any partner would have to support her in that ambition.

Chapter 13

In her quest to learn more about Mark's character, Jean accepted his persistent offers to take her to lunch or to various local entertainment venues. He picked her up one Saturday morning and drove her to his parents' palatial home on the outskirts of Punting to meet his mother, Lady Mary Raeburn. Jean was rather nervous at the prospect and thought it was too early in her relationship with Mark to make the acquaintance of other members of his family, but she acceded to his request.

In contrast to Mark's father's blunt Yorkshire manner, Lady Mary was effusive, greeting Jean with a torrent of welcoming words that were almost embarrassing. It was evident that she had a powerful personality that bordered on pretentiousness. Jean instantly knew where Mark's overconfident bearing came from. Moreover, it was clear that his mother adored him and was willing to forgive his recklessness and his casual approach to life. She had ignored his failed grades at university and supported him in any battles with his father, always ensuring that he received his monthly allowance. It was surprising that she was happy about his feelings for Jean, but she was confident that she would have dominance over any other woman that came into his life. Jean, who was just a primary school teacher from an ordinary family, was no exception. Jean said goodbye to Lady Mary with some relief after receiving another exuberant kiss on her left cheek.

On the drive back to the restaurant where they had previously eaten, Mark casually asked Jean her opinion of his mother. She merely commented that she was a very nice lady with a warm personality and that she was obviously very fond of him.

During the lunch, Mark looked at Jean and said rather embarrassedly, "I have reflected about our conversation in my car on the evening of the annual dance, and I have spoken to my father about giving him some active support with his business affairs. He was pleased about that but told me that in order to learn about the management of the business, I would have to start at the bottom, and that includes knowledge of the cement works and the limestone quarry."

Jean remarked, "I think that is fair, Mark. You will probably learn more working with the men in the quarry than you will in your dad's office. You will see the arduous conditions and the risks they undertake every day."

Mark frowned and exclaimed, "But I did not go to uni just to end up doing manual labour. I do not mind helping out occasionally doing some administration, but that is all."

Jean looked Mark squarely in the eye.

"How do you think your father began? He did not inherit his businesses! He started from scratch, working down on the quarry face as a miner. It took hard effort to get where he is today, and he has earned his reward. He wants you to do the same so that you appreciate not only what you have but what it took to give it to you."

Mark grunted, not looking very pleased.

"I will think about it."

Jean nodded. "All right, Mark, but please understand that though I am attracted to you, I will not stay with you if you continue with your feckless ways. My father worked all his life in the quarry and still does, even though he could have retired after his lung tumour was discovered. I love him, but I also respect him for his sense of responsibility for my mother and me. Now, you have taken me to your home, and you have visited mine, so please let me take you round my village and show you some of the places where I spent my childhood."

Jean directed a somewhat subdued Mark to Bucton's main parade of shops, which included the grocery store, the stationers and newsagents and the post office, known locally as the Meeting Place where Maisie Parsons held court, delivering the latest gossip with postage stamps and pension payments. Jean noted with some surprise that the post office, usually busy on a Saturday, was closed. She wondered if Maisie had caught a bug and was suffering at home. At least, libellous rumours would stop circulating until her return to work.

Jean pointed out Tom Sharpe's butchery shop with the abattoir at the rear. Her father, who always enjoyed a pun, suggested that the premises should also be known as the Meat in Place. Mark showed no interest in this fanciful information, so Jean guided him down to the primary school where she spent so many hours educating and inspiring youngsters to reach their potential. Her companion nodded as she commented on the latent talent shown by some of her pupils but remained silent.

Jean suddenly realised that his previous ebullient mood had been darkened by her earlier chastisement. She had thought of taking him to the meadow and strolling along the river where she and Ben had learned to swim, but there was no point in doing that while he was reflecting on the ultimatum that she had given him. He readily acquiesced when she asked him to take her home, making a headache an excuse. She gave him a light kiss as he dropped her off outside Wisteria Cottage and then watched as he drove away without saying anything further to her. She wondered if she would ever see him again.

Chapter 14

Two days later, Maisie Parsons' body was found in the river close to where Jean had intended to take Mark. Forensic examination revealed a large bloody indentation on the back of her skull. On the bank nearby, a rock was stained with congealed blood. Her lungs held water which indicated that she was still alive when she fell or was pushed into the river.

Although the death of the postmistress was a shock to the community, very few people mourned her loss. Her continual interference in residents' lives and her rumour spreading had angered many in the village, and she had acquired several enemies due to her malicious gossiping. If her death was the result of a crime, there were many suspects who could have committed it.

There was no police station at Bucton, so the investigation into Maisie's death was conducted by the CID based in Punting. Searches at the post office and her home revealed nothing that would link her demise to any one individual. The riverbank and the meadow were scoured for evidence that a personal struggle between Maisie and an attacker had taken place. House-to-house interviews in the village produced the names of residents who may have had a grudge against the postmistress because of her indiscretions, but there were no positive leads.

Enquiries continued for many weeks but concluded with no definite result; had she stumbled and fallen back so that she hit her head on the rock and lost consciousness? Had she staggered up, lost her footing while still dazed and tumbled off the bank into the river, or had she been struck from behind by an unknown assailant and then thrown into the water?

The coroner returned an open verdict, and the case was put on file. Another postmistress was appointed, and life in the village returned to normal.

Jean did not hear from Mark during this period and became quite concerned about his silence, though she thought it best not to contact him directly. It was up to him to decide whether he wanted to continue their relationship or carry on with his thriftless life. She was dangerously attracted to him, but she would not abandon her moral principles in order to be with him. She knew that she would feel deep disappointment if he was unwilling to change his rakish ways for her sake. Marriage was a long way off unless he assumed a more responsible attitude in finding suitable employment which would allow her to continue with her teaching career. In the meantime, she had to care for her parents. Her mother was becoming more detached from reality, and Jean feared that Alzheimer's disease was beginning to develop. She spoke to her father about her concern.

"I know, Jean. I am also worried about her, but she will not talk to me. She is very argumentative when I attempt to discuss anything with her. It seems that she blames me for your brother's death. The doctors told me that meningitis is the result of a bacterial or viral infection, and once it reached Simon's brain there was little hope for him. I grieved for him too, and I am sure you would have liked to have a younger brother, but we had no choice except to accept his loss and move on with our lives. Sadly, your mother has not been able to. I expect she will only get worse as she ages, Jean, so what can we do about it? I cannot afford full-time professional care for her, and I cannot expect you to give up your teaching post since I know how much it means to you. I suppose that I could retire from my job at the quarry to look after her, but I doubt if she would allow me. I love her deeply, Jean, but I do not have a patient temperament that would allow me to accept her constant rebukes. She would probably refuse to take the medication I give her. What do you think we should do?"

After much discussion between Jean and her father, they decided to employ a qualified carer to stay with the ailing parent during Jean's school hours and Henry's work period up at the quarry. Jean would take over from the carer at about 4pm each day. Payment would come from their joint income, though it would stretch the household budget. Jean said she would advertise for a suitable female carer who had a friendly disposition and was conscientious and reliable.

It occurred to Jean that even if Mark had wanted to resume their relationship on her terms, she would not be able to spend much time with him because of her added commitment to her mother. She shrugged her shoulders. Her parents had sacrificed a lot to bring her up and pay for her to go to teaching college to fulfil her dream. Now it was payback time.

Chapter 15

Three weeks later, Jean received a telephone call from Mark. Her heartbeat quickened when she heard his voice, but then she held her breath with worry at what he would say to her.

"Jean, I thought you would like to know that I accepted my father's conditions of employment, and I will be working down at the quarry from next week. I am not looking forward to it, but I will give it a go. Will you come out to lunch and help me commiserate?"

Jean almost let out a shriek of delight despite Mark's reluctant tone but controlled herself and replied quite calmly, "Yes, of course, Mark, but it will have to be at the weekend. I am back at school now."

"That's fine, Jean. I will pick you up on Sunday just before midday. We will dine at our usual restaurant. Is that OK?"

Jean assured him that she would be looking forward to the luncheon, told him that she was pleased with his decision and rang off. With her mother enclosed in her room, Jean felt the freedom to twirl around the sitting room, dancing with joyous movement before collapsing into one of the armchairs. She caught sight of her glowing face in the mirror on the wall above the hearth. She looked like a young teenager instead of a 25-year-old schoolteacher. She could not wait until Sunday.

Mark picked her up as planned, complimenting her on the new dress she had bought for the occasion. Jean was pleased that he had noticed it.

At the restaurant, waiting for their meal to be served, he looked across at her and exclaimed, "I have missed seeing you, Jean, and I have been seriously considering the comments you made during our previous chats. I realise that I have been drifting through life without much purpose since coming down from uni. I still do not know which direction to take in the way of a career, but I know that I must settle on something. I am not thrilled at working for my father at the quarry, but you are right that as his son I should try to assist him in his businesses. I would have preferred it if he had installed me in a comfortable office and just allowed me to deal administratively with his commercial affairs, though no doubt I would have soon died of boredom unless I had you as my personal assistant!"

Jean smiled.

"I am afraid that would not be possible, Mark. I am committed to my teaching career, and that will not change. I get a lot of satisfaction from teaching young children."

Mark felt compelled to ask the question, "What about marriage, Jean? Have you never thought about getting married and having children of your own?"

"Yes, of course, Mark. My father has asked me the same thing. I am still young, and I need to find the right sort of man who would always be supportive of me and be a responsible husband and father."

"What about love, Jean? Is that not important, too?"

Jean nodded emphatically.

"I could not marry any man I did not love or who did not love me, but mutual respect is also needed for any marriage to survive."

The first course of their meal arrived, and there was a pause in the conversation. Jean finally broke the silence.

"What is happening tomorrow, Mark? Is your father taking you down to the quarry in the morning? Do you know what he expects you to do?"

"I would imagine that he would introduce me to the site manager, who will be asked to escort me round the quarry. I have never been down there, so I have no idea what to expect."

"I am sure that you will get to chat with some of the work crew, Mark, but my dad will be up in his office at the top of the quarry, so he will be happy to answer any questions you have. I do not expect you will be doing much manual work for a while. There will be a lot to learn. Please ring me at home after school hours because I will want to hear your thoughts on the day's experience."

"Yes, of course I will, Jean, though do not expect me to be elated. I would much rather be spending the day with you."

Jean smiled.

"You need to start somewhere, Mark, and it may not be as bad as you may think. Let us enjoy this evening together, and this time I will join you in a glass of wine."

Chapter 16

At his father's bidding, Mark was taken at 8am into the depths of the limestone quarry clad in a hard hat, steel toe-capped boots and working protective clothing. He was shocked by its depth and breadth, gouged out of the ground during past centuries. It was akin to a huge open cavern, with the walls towering skywards to a height of a thousand metres. Mark felt dwarfed by the vastness.

The site manager escorted him around and gave him a brief history of the quarry, which had been bought by Sir John Raeburn after it had been abandoned due to its unprofitability. Two world wars had drained it of its manpower and lowered its output. Mark's father, seeing its potential with the increase in the construction industry following the end of WWII, had seized the opportunity to buy it from the former owners at a bargain price. At the same time, he bought the adjoining cement works and re-employed the local quarrymen who had returned from active war service. The Great Rocks railway, which was part of the Midland Rail system, was upgraded to allow stone freight trains to run through the quarry to Bucton and other parts of the Peak District of Derbyshire and beyond to deliver the limestone to the yards of building companies. Within a short time, the quarry and cement works had returned to profitability and provided the main income for the male residents of Bucton and the surrounding towns and villages.

Mark rang Jean that evening as promised. He told her that her assumption was correct, that the day would not be as bad as he had feared. He had been an observer of the activities most of the time, but he had been interested in what he had seen. It was obvious that he had a lot to learn, but he hoped to have an informative chat with her father on the morrow up in the quarry hut.

Jean was delighted to hear the news. It pleased her that though he had previously shown no enthusiasm for working at the open mine, he was willing to go back the next day to acquire more knowledge. She mentioned Mark's intention to her father, who commented that he was glad that Sir John's son had finally decided to take an interest in the business and he would look forward to their chat. Neither he nor his daughter were aware that Mark's sudden turnaround may have been due to the possible loss of his father's monthly allowance.

The next day the site manager increased Mark's scant education about limestone and its various uses in the construction industry. He explained that limestone was a common type of carbonate sedimentary rock comprised of calcium, magnesium and other minerals and was formed in shallow marine environments from bedrock sediments deposited on earth over millions of years. It proved that England had long lain under water before the seas subsided. Fossils of extinct animals had been uncovered during the excavation of deep quarries, together with molluscs such as whelks, clams, scallops and oysters. Found in the grains of limestone were skeletal fragments of other marine organisms such as squid and octopus, cuttlefish, slugs and snails. Mark was intrigued by this information and wanted to know more. Later that day, Jean's father provided it.

Chapter 17

Henry Stanley had been a quarryman all his life and had studied the history of limestone back to Roman times. Sitting beside Mark in the little hut perched high up on the lip of the quarry, he told the younger man about the architectural revolution instigated by the Roman Emperor Augusta in the first century AD. It was Augusta who used lime and volcanic ash hydrated with seawater to rebuild the city of Rome, constructing amphitheatres, aqueducts, bridges and dams in concrete. In Athens he built the Pantheon, which today still has the world's largest unreinforced solid concrete dome. He was also responsible for the building of the Acropolis and was the very first to design arches, vaults and domes using limestone. His method of construction was far more difficult without machinery, but while modern concrete can crack after a few years, his architecture has survived with no detectable fault.

Mark was fascinated by the extent of Henry's knowledge. He had never shown much interest in history, considering the present and the future more important, particularly in his relationship with Jean, but he suddenly realised that without the events of the past, the world would be a different place. Evolution had played its part, but so had human influence. Not always for the better, he had to admit.

Henry asked Mark if he knew the full extent of the commercial usefulness of limestone and its aggregates. Obviously, he knew about its part in constructing bricks and building blocks and modern paving and road making, but was he aware that calcium carbonate extracted from limestone was used in toothpaste products or paint, and even as a soil conditioner to neutralise acidic soil which permits the growth of certain crops? No, he did not. Mark confessed his ignorance. Did he also not know that before electricity was invented, lime was burnt to create light in theatres so the players could perform before their audience? It resulted in the term 'Being in the limelight'. That fact surprised Mark, and he asked Jean if she had known that during a telephone call asking her out to supper.

"No, Mark, I did not, but I do remember seeing the film *Limelight,* produced by and starring Charlie Chaplin. I thought that was quite good. Yes, I will come out for supper with you as your reward for your second day at the quarry and for listening to my father. I have homework to check and evaluate first, but I should be ready in about an hour or so. Can you pick me up about 7.30pm?"

Sitting with Mark in the Moon and Sixpence licensed public house in Bucton's town centre, Jean sipped a small glass of white wine and asked her companion about his conversations with the quarry manager and her father. More importantly, was he interested enough to know more about the limestone industry, or had he been bored?

Mark smiled.

"Yes, I expected to be, and to be honest with you, when I was first taken into the quarry, I wanted to be anywhere else except there. It is not the most attractive of places, and I yearned to be on a golf course or a tennis court. Strangely though, in listening to the site manager and then your father, I became interested in the history of the limestone rock, the methods used in its extraction and the minerals and fossils that can be found in it. It occurred to me that geology or an environmental science linked to it may be a career worth following."

Jean outstretched a hand and touched Mark on his right arm.

Softly but earnestly, she said, "Mark, I am so pleased to hear that. It may be what you have been looking for since coming down from university, a career that would give you a feeling of fulfilment. You could not continue following an aimless path. You may gain temporary pleasure from it, but in the end, you will ask yourself what lasting satisfaction you have gained from it."

Mark gazed back at Jean. Her concern for his future and the eagerness with which she expressed her desire to see him change his wayward lifestyle amazed him. Who was this woman who stirred his blood so much that he was willing to do anything to please her? Yes, she was a very attractive woman with a natural beauty that needed no artificial enhancement, but under the skin was a firmness of character that would not yield to any behaviour that challenged the high principles she had set herself. Could he match those moral standards in order to have a lasting, loving relationship with her? He was not sure, but he was willing to try. He leaned across the table, took the wine glass out of her hand and placed it on the table.

"Jean. We have known each other for just a short while, but I am attracted to you, and I would like to have a steady relationship with you. You have an honesty about you that I like, and your candour is a refreshing change from the flattery I get from people who want to befriend me because I am the son of Sir Joshua Raeburn. I am not the reprobate that I am rumoured to be, but it is certainly true that I have done nothing to improve the frivolous reputation I have. If you are willing to continue our friendship and allow me to escort you to social events when you are not engaged at the primary school, I will continue working at the quarry. Whether that will inspire me into studying ecology or geology, only time will tell, but if it does I am sure my father will be pleased."

"And so will I," Jean murmured, "and of course we can remain friends."

Chapter 18

When the telephone rang around 6pm the next Friday evening, Jean was sitting in the lounge marking homework. Her father picked the instrument up and listened to the caller before holding it out to her.

"It's Mark Raeburn, Jean. Do you want to speak to him?"

"Yes, Father. I will take it on the extension in my bedroom so you will not be disturbed listening to your sport on the wireless."

In her room, she sat on the edge of her bed and picked up the receiver. She waited until she heard a click as her father replaced the downstairs telephone.

"Hullo, Mark! How are you?"

She tried to keep the excitement mounting as the deep tone of his voice reached her.

"I am fine, Jean, thanks, but I have had a busy week in the quarry. I wondered if you would like to accompany me for a drive over the weekend. I think that I must have swallowed quite a lot of gritstone dust in the last few days, and I need to clear my lungs and breathe in some clean air!"

"Where were you thinking of going, Mark?"

"It will have to be somewhere in the Peak District, Jean, as we will only have a day and a half if I pick you up in the morning. You will have to go back to your school on Monday, and my father will expect me down in the quarry. The forecast for this weekend is quite good, so I can take you on a tour of interesting places that I know."

"That will be fine, Mark. I have not seen as much of my home county as I would have liked. Is there anything that I should take with me?"

There was a slight hesitation before Mark's reply.

"I suggest you bring an overnight bag, as we may wish to attend an evening performance at a theatre in one of the towns which may end quite late. It would be convenient to book into a hotel for the night and continue our tour in the morning after breakfast."

Jean's heart lurched in disappointment and disquiet at Mark's suggestion. Previously, he had honestly admitted to her that he had been wanton in his past behaviour, but he had also expressed a desire to cast off his footloose and fancy-free reputation and do something more purposeful with his life. Was he now reverting to type? Did he believe that he could seduce her so easily? Was that the reason for his invitation to show the rural delights of Derbyshire?

As calmly as she could, she replied, "I am not sure that is a good idea, Mark. I think I would like to sleep in my own bed if you don't mind driving me back to Bucton tomorrow evening."

There was silence at the other end of the phone while Mark digested her answer. Then she heard a chuckle of amusement.

"Jean, you misunderstand me! I was not thinking of booking a double room for us! I am not that shameless! I will book two single rooms and ensure that yours has an interior lock on the door so that you will feel safe from any unwanted advances."

When there was no response to this assurance, Mark hastily continued, "Although I would have driven you back home if you had asked me to, it would have been a waste of time and effort. We could have set off early from the hotel on Sunday morning to tour other parts of the Peak District. One place I would like to drive you to is Hope Valley and to the little village of Hope. Like many other villages in Derbyshire, it is mentioned in the Domesday Book and has not only survived the last one thousand years but has thrived economically because of the limestone rock it sits upon. Visiting Hope with you will encourage me to think of a happy and prosperous future."

There was a moment's silence before Jean's response.

"Mark, we all need hope and optimism in our lives to motivate us to reach our desired goals and to ward off any feelings of despair. Without those positive emotions, we are all lost souls and will never find contentment in anything. Of course, hope by itself is not enough, but if it is combined with a determination to improve any bad situation that we may find ourselves in, we will win through. I do have faith that you will find the right course to follow which will provide personal satisfaction and the respect of other people around you. In doing so you will also find self-respect. Yes, Mark, thank you, I will accept your invitation based on our agreed conditions, and I shall look forward to visiting Hope Valley. I should be ready around 9am. Goodnight, Mark. Happy dreams."

Jean replaced the receiver and allowed herself to fall back on the bed so that her head rested on the soft pillows. With arms outstretched on either side of the white coverlet, she gazed up at the ceiling. A smile lit up her face, and a warm glow spread throughout her body as she concentrated her thoughts on Mark.

The rasping sound of a cough from the room below disturbed her reverie. Reluctantly she stood up, smoothed her dress and went downstairs. Her father was still sitting in his armchair with the television switched off.

"Are you alright, Father?" she asked. "I heard you cough."

"Yes, but I am OK, Jean. Don't worry. I think I swallowed some air that made me gag. What did Mark want?"

"He offered to take me for a drive around the county tomorrow. I accepted. I hope you don't mind."

"No, Jean. I trust your judgement, but I suggest that you do not tell your mother as I doubt if you will get her approval."

Henry forced himself out of his chair.

"I think I will go down to the Pig and Whistle for an hour if you are going to stay in and finish checking those exercise books. Just pop in to see if your mother needs anything while I am gone."

Jean nodded.

"Go and have a pint with your workmates, Dad. I will keep an eye on Mother."

She watched him walk down the garden path with slow, uneven steps. He cut a sad and lonely figure as he opened the gate and headed in the direction of the local inn. She thought about her conversation with Mark. Her most steadfast hope was the restoration of the loving bond her parents had enjoyed over the years, and which had sustained her during her childhood. It grieved her now to see the gap that had opened between them since the death of her young brother. It must be so difficult for her father dealing with her mother's rejection of him. Jean knew how much he loved her, and his heart must be tearing apart.

Chapter 19

Mark arrived promptly at 9am the next morning. Jean greeted him at the cottage door with a small suitcase in one hand and a picnic hamper basket in the other. Smilingly, she held them both out.

"Good morning, Mark! It is such a fine day I thought we could sit and have an alfresco lunch under a tree somewhere. Can you put my case and the hamper at the back, please?"

"What a splendid idea, Jean. Yes, of course. The Peak District is full of hills and dales with wonderful views, so you will have lots of choices where you wish to stop for our midday snack. I have written a list of interesting places you may like to see apart from Hope Valley."

Mark continued, "Do you agree that we should first head for Castleton, since it has two first-class hotels? You can decide in which one you would like us to book our single rooms for tonight. With the reservation settled, we have the whole day and part of tomorrow to explore as much of the county as you want."

"Yes, Mark, that is fine. You know the county better than I do. I will look at your list, but I will leave it to you to drive us to those places that you think would be of the greatest interest to me."

She smiled across at him as she buckled her seatbelt.

"Right, Mark. I am in your hands."

The drive to Chapel-en-le Frith, a small village on the boundary of the Peak District National Park, sitting in a valley between rolling hills, took less than twenty minutes. It was previously a heavily wooded area used as a private hunting ground by William the First. Occupied by the Normans in the

12th century, its name translated into Chapel in the Forest. Jean had learned that it was the first settlement in the Peak District founded by the Picts, who had spread from Scotland and the northern borders into that part of Derbyshire and the surrounding areas. The name Peak District had nothing to do with the numerous mountain tops in that area but had derived from the tribal Picts that occupied it.

The main point of interest in the village for Jean was the Church of St. Thomas Becket, built and named by the Normans after the invasion of England in 1066. Becket was the Archbishop of Canterbury martyred in the cathedral in 1170. His parents were of Norman stock, which may explain the building of this church a long way from his diocese.

Mark surprised Jean by mentioning that on previous visits to the village he had been told that Will Scarlett, a former member of legendary Robin Hood's band of Merry Men, had died in Chapel-en-le-Frith in December 1283. That could have been factually correct. Sherwood Forest in the neighbouring county of Nottinghamshire was not that far distant; Scarlett's birthplace had not been recorded, so it could have been in the Derbyshire village. English medieval folklore is filled with tales and ballads about the yeoman outlaw Robin Hood, Maid Marion, Friar Tuck, Little John and all the other men that fought against the taxes imposed by the Sheriff of Nottingham while King Richard I, known as the Lionheart, was away on the Crusades.

Chapter 20

Mark drove on through open moorland towards a village called Dove Holes, explaining to Jean that he often came to shoot red grouse in the season between August and December. Jean confessed that she had never eaten this game bird, which is considered a delicacy by the wealthy. Although she was not a vegetarian, she objected to the hunting and killing of any wildlife for sport. Her companion remained silent on hearing this comment. Feeling his discomfort, Jean changed the subject.

"The guidebook mentions that there are several limestone quarries in this area. Is that the reason you want to visit Dove Holes?"

Mark nodded. "Yes, your father suggested that if I am interested in becoming an ecologist, I should visit as many quarries as I can. Apart from that, I believe that near here is an ancient site called the Bull Ring, which is similar to Stonehenge, though on a smaller scale, and knowing your interest in history, I thought that you would like to visit it."

"Oh, Mark, that is thoughtful of you. Yes, I would! The guide mentions it but also explains the reason the village is called Dove Holes. Did you know that the word Dove comes from the Celtic Welsh word 'dwr', which means water? It explains why the south-eastern port of Dover is so named."

Mark admitted that he did not.

"I am surprised, Jean, since Dover is nowhere near Wales, but I will accept your word for it."

Mark took the steep drive up the Hope Valley to Castleton, passing through the towering limestone hills which enclosed the narrow winding gorge known as Winnats Pass.

Looking northwards, Jean could see the sloping 517-metre hill known as Mam Tor, which had earned the alternative name Shivering Mountain on account of the continual landslides on the eastern side caused by loose shale. She was later to learn that at its base stand four deep caverns that date back to the Stone Age and are regular tourist sites. Fossilised human remains from the Neolithic period have been discovered, while stalagmites and stalactites hung from the cavern roofs like icy ornaments decorated by ancient cave dwellers. In more recent times, the limestone walls had been deeply dug in order to extract the mineral content that, when separated, play a vital role in industry and the field of medicine. In two of the caverns, namely the Blue Stone and the Treak Cliff, a crystallised mineral with ornamental colouring has been extracted and used for items of jewellery. The Treak cavern, at least 1000ft in length, has several separate show caves, each individually named, i.e., Aladdin, Fairyland, the Dome of St Paul's, the Dream Cave and the Witches Cave.

Mark continued the drive until they reached Castleton, an ancient settlement mentioned in the Domesday Book of 1086 and the centre of the lead mining industry. Lead was used extensively for thousands of years until its poisonous elements were recognised and the lead mines were abandoned. Castleton is now known for its cement works and its situation in the plateau between the Dark Peak and the White Peak moorland areas of Derbyshire.

Mark's guidebook explained that on the 29th May each year, known throughout the country as Oak Apple Day, the town holds a procession through the town in early evening which commemorates the 17th-century re-establishment of Charles II to the throne after the death of Oliver Cromwell in 1658. Charles escaped from the defeat by Cromwell's Roundheads of his forces in the Battle of Worcester, which ended the Civil War in 1651. Pursued by Cromwell's army, he hid in an apple tree in the gardens of Boscobel Abbey in Shropshire during his eventual successful flight to France. In re-enacting the escape from the apple tree on each anniversary, a local man representing the king rides through Castleton on horseback wearing a beehive-shaped wicker-framed garland of oak apple leaves and floristry over his head and body, followed on foot by most of the townsfolk wearing sprigs of apple leaves in support of Charles II. Those who do not are chastised by having their rear ends pinched; hence the unofficial name for the day became "Pinch-Bum Day".

High on the hill above Castleton sits the ruins of Peveril Castle, a fortification whose history was well known to Jean because of her love of Shakespeare. It was built by a Norman knight and a follower of William the Conqueror. It eventually fell into the hands of John of Gaunt, the Duke of Lancaster. Shakespeare wrote about him in his play Richard II. These immortal words, "this blessed plot, this earth, this England", are part of a speech attributed to John of Gaunt by England's greatest bard.

Jean was thrilled to see the castle and asked Mark if they could get a closer view of it. He nodded.

"Yes, if you wish. It is just a pile of old stones and not of much interest to me, but your wish is my command. Can we book into a hotel first, though, and have a meal? I am quite peckish!"

Ninety minutes later and booked into two rooms in a hotel in the town centre, Jean looked at Mark across the dining table in the main restaurant.

"Thank you, Mark. It has been an interesting drive so far. I am looking forward to where you may take me for the rest of the day."

"Jean, it is my pleasure to escort you around. There are lots of places in this area of Derbyshire that I have driven through without paying much attention to them, but having you sitting beside me and commenting on different sites that have attracted you will make the drive far more interesting. I want to visit Hope Village for the reason I explained to you, but we could walk there from Castleton if you wish. Perhaps after breakfast in the morning?"

Jean smiled at his quizzical countenance, noting the brow that was furrowed with anxiety. This was not the confident man that she was used to seeing.

"Yes, of course, Mark."

Chapter 21

Having refreshed themselves and changed into stouter clothing, Mark and Jean attempted the steep climb to Peveril Castle. Mark was not too keen on that idea, but Jean persuaded him to make the effort. Slowly and carefully, and taking an easier route shown in a guidebook that Jean had bought, it took just over an hour to reach the top of the western edge. The view over the sheer face far exceeded their expectations. A stunning panorama lay before them. Jean was mesmerised by the scene and involuntarily put her arms around Mark's waist. He responded by kissing her on the top of her head while they gazed silently at the wild but spectacular landscape. Finally, they managed to direct their attention to the ruins of the castle. There was no doubt that its location had been chosen for its defensive position overlooking miles of the Peak District. Founded after the Norman conquest of 1066, it guarded that area of Derbyshire against opposing armies of Picts and Anglo-Saxons. It eventually fell into disuse, and little of the main structure remains.

Carefully navigating their way down to Castleton with Mark leading, the pair sat on an outcrop of rock to catch their breath. Jean realised that the climb had taken more energy than she thought it would. She looked at her companion and smiled.

"You must be fitter than I am, Mark! When I get back to school, I will have to join some of the pupils in their cross-country runs to reduce my waistline!"

Mark looked at her figure appreciatively.

"No need for that, Jean. You look fine to me. I would not want to see you differently to your present shape."

He held out a hand to assist her to stand, pretending not to notice that his comment had flushed her cheeks even more than they already were. He continued, "Shall we get a drink somewhere? I am feeling quite parched."

Slowly they walked towards the café in Castleton High St. As they prepared to enter, Jean clutched Mark's arm and exclaimed, "I forgot. My hamper is in your car!"

"No problem, Jean. I am sure that the food is well wrapped up, so it will keep. We can enjoy our picnic later after we have visited Hope. Meanwhile, you can rest and enjoy a cup of tea before we take the walk down to the village. That is if you are up to it, of course!"

Inside the café, a pot of tea was ordered. It arrived with a small plate of mixed scones. To Mark's chagrin, no wine was available. He smiled across the table at Jean as she poured out a cup of tea for him and offered a scone.

"I am not used to this, Jean! My order is usually a half bottle of full-bodied French wine with a sirloin roast."

"Sorry, Mark! I am afraid that if you stay with me, you will have to get used to more mundane fare. I need to live within my means. But don't worry, I have a roast chicken in the hamper with a bottle of Chianti. You can indulge yourself another time."

Mark took a reluctant sip of his black tea, no sugar.

"It's fine. Jean. Being with you is a price worth paying."

Jean changed the subject.

"Where will you take me after we have visited Hope, Mark?"

"We will have plenty of time afterwards. The whole of the Peak District is full of interest and scenic beauty, Jean, and there are historic places for you to look at, but I think you may like to visit Edale, which lies down the valley. It is the start of the Pennine Way, so though it is a small village, it is always full of tourists making their way through it to Scotland. Afterwards, we can have our picnic in one of the dales."

Chapter 22

Strolling hand in hand and following the stream that flowed through Castleton to Hope, which Jean later learned was called Peakshole Water, the walk to the village took around half an hour. They paused briefly outside to read the inscriptions on the First World War memorial before moving on to St Peter's Church, erected in the 14th century. They found a Saxon monument and evidence of a Roman settlement. Mark was more interested in the 17th-century dwellings and the few modern houses which had been constructed from gritstone. Since the village of Hope had survived medieval times, including the Bronze Age, it was named appropriately. Jean was determined to research more of Hope's history when she returned home because it would inspire her if she ever had doubts about her future.

Retracing their steps back to Castleton, the couple drove to Edale, which lay within a small, forested area a few miles northwest. As Mark had previously commented, the village bustled with tourists trekking through with rucksacks on their backs heading for the Pennine Way. Edale marked the beginning of the 268-mile official trail to the Scottish border. On average, that arduous journey takes about three days and even longer in bad weather conditions that challenge the hardiest of ramblers. Fortunately, there are camping sites and lodges on the way, and steps have been cut out by local farmers on the steepest climb towards the end of the route. These steps became known as Jacob's Ladder, alternatively the Stairway to Heaven. Mark suggested with tongue in cheek that Jean might like to join other ramblers on this trek during one of her school breaks. She responded with the hope that if she did so, he may like to accompany her.

Mark shook his head.

"That is too much of a challenge for me, Jean. I will happily drive up to meet you at the finishing point, though!"

Jean laughed to hide her disappointment and then said teasingly, "I thought climbing the Stairway to Heaven may have motivated you! Never mind. Perhaps I can get you to change your mind once you have toughened up working in the quarry! Anyway, let us explore the village, and then you can drive me to a beauty spot where we can picnic."

The Old Nag's Head in the village was their first point of call. They refreshed themselves with tonic water while chatting with the landlord, who informed them that the pub had once been a Smithy and dated back to 1577. On mentioning their short visit to Hope, he commented that the road between Edale and Castleton in times gone by when there was no church or cemetery in Edale, had been known as 'Coffin Road', since the deceased residents had been transported along that route on the way to Hope for their funeral and burial.

Mark and Jean walked around the village for a while but were constantly hampered by tourists. The decision was made to drive out to a less crowded area. An hour later, Mark parked on top of a hill that gave a splendid view of the Derwent Valley. Beside the chosen picnic spot, a growing clump of a blue flower caught Jean's eye. She recognised it as a perennial plant that grew in her father's garden. She was later to learn that it was the adopted plant of Derbyshire. Its botanical name is Polemonium, otherwise known as Jacob's Ladder.

Thoughts of her father prompted Jean to wonder if he was having a good day alone with her mother or whether she had shut herself away from him again. As she spread out the picnic blanket on the ground while Mark was lifting the hamper out of the car, she decided that she would discuss the strained relationship between her parents with him. It was right that he should be acquainted with the situation since it impacted on their own relationship. She sat in thoughtful silence for a while, gazing down on the panorama below. Beside her, a hungry Mark was already devouring chicken and ham with gusto in between sips of the wine.

She reached out a hand and touched him lightly on his sleeve.

"Mark," she said falteringly. "I need to tell you something."

He turned to her.

"What is the matter, Jean? Why are you not eating? I thought that you were enjoying this day out?"

"Yes, I am, Mark. Very much so, but this has nothing to do with it. I want to talk to you about my parents."

"Oh, I see, or perhaps I don't. I am not sure whether the relationship between your parents is any business of mine but go ahead. I am listening. I like your father. He is a blunt, straight-talking, honest man that does not mince his words, and he certainly knows a lot about quarrying. He taught me quite a lot when we had our chat up in the hut. However, I did detect some sadness in him, for whatever reason I do not know. As for your mother, I must admit that I felt a chilliness about her when we met. No doubt she had picked up some gossip about me in the village."

Jean nodded in agreement.

"That is correct, Mark. She does disapprove of you, based on what she has been told about you. My father has no great prejudice against you and always forms his own opinions. That is not what I want to talk about. Both my parents are estranged now, which is the reason for my father's sadness. Ever since the death of my baby brother Simon, my mother has shut herself off from my father and will not even talk to him. She is suffering from melancholia and needs psychiatric help to lift her out of the despair. More than that, she needs someone with her all the time in case she thinks about self-harming. I do not want my dad to give up his job in the quarry because he enjoys it so much, and obviously, I do not want to give up my teaching career."

"So, what is it that you are asking me, Jean? I do not think I am qualified to give advice on neurosis. If I can help with funding a carer for your mother while you and your father are actively engaged from home, I can possibly do that."

"No, no, Mark! I would not dream of asking you to do that! I am trying to explain to you that I may have less time to see you since I may need to stay at home after school hours in order to look after Mother when any carer has left. She disregards anything my father says or tries to do. For some unfathomable reason, she blames him for Simon's death."

"Oh."

Mark's disappointment was palpable. He sat in silence, staring down at the scenic view. Suddenly, it did not look so beautiful.

He turned to Jean.

"I hoped that we would spend more time together, not less. It seems pointless working in the quarry if I am not able to see you. I think I have fallen in love with you."

Jean was saddened by his doleful expression. She tightened her grip on his arm and quickly responded.

"No, no, Mark. I have deep feelings for you too, and I would love to have a long-lasting relationship with you, but only if you buckle down and work towards a worthwhile career. You showed an interest in Geology, but you can choose what you wish to do. In the meantime, I have a sense of duty towards my mother that I cannot ignore. Hopefully, circumstances may change, and Mother's mental health will improve so that my parents can resume their loving relationship. I will always be supportive of you, and we can get together again. I am sure that in time my mother will gain a more positive view of your character if she sees that you are in active employment."

Mark sighed.

"Alright, Jean. I will do as you ask and go back to the quarry on Monday. At least I will have the pleasure of your company for one more day."

Chapter 23

Mark dropped Jean off the next evening outside her parents' cottage, still looking despondent. He had been very quiet on the final day, though Jean tried to cheer him up as he drove to different parts of the county. A peck on his cheek did little to lighten his spirits, and he drove away from her unsmilingly. Jean sighed as she carried the travelling case and hamper into the house. It was not how she wanted the day to end.

Her father looked up from the book he was reading. He smiled and asked her if she had enjoyed the weekend excursion.

"Yes, Dad. It was very interesting. How have you been? How is Mother?"

"Alright, I think, Jean. She has hardly come out of her room, but she did eat the food that I took into her. I tried to talk to her, but she kept gazing out of the window and not replying. I am really concerned about her."

"Don't worry, Dad. I will go in to see her in a few minutes. Would you like a cup of tea?"

"No thanks, Jean. Now you are here, I think that I will go up to bed. I am rather tired. I am glad that you had a good time. You can tell me all about it tomorrow."

He smiled at his daughter, put down his book and stood up. Jean kissed him on his forehead before watching him leave the room. She went into the kitchen, made two cups of tea and went into her mother's bedroom. She was sitting in an armchair, looking out of the window that faced the front garden. One of the Agatha Christie novels was upturned on her lap.

"Hello, Mother," she said as gaily as she could. "I have brought you a cup of tea."

Ann Stanley turned her head. "Thank you, Jean. Have you been out today?"

"Yes, Mother. I have been for a drive. I needed some fresh air after being in school all week. You could have come with me if you had wanted."

She knew that her mother would have declined the offer.

"I am more comfortable here, Jean. I don't really want to go out anymore. You can tuck me into bed if you like. Your father offered, but I don't want him touching me."

Jean shook her head. Very softly she said, not wishing to anger her parent, "Mother, Father loves you. He always has. He is distraught that you blame him for Simon's death."

Ann's bitter tone shook her daughter.

"And so he was. I will never forgive him for letting my baby die. Now, please help me into bed. I do not want to talk about it."

Jean did as she was bid and left the room with tears in her eyes. Would nothing ever change her mother's mind?

Chapter 24

Jean did not hear from Mark for several days and concluded that he had accepted that her evenings and weekends were committed to caring for her mother. Her father had confirmed that Mark had returned to his daily task in the quarry. She was pleased with that news and was even more pleased when he met her outside the school gates two weeks later at the end of lessons.

Most of the pupils had left the school buildings to go home, but one or two were still chatting outside. They glanced curiously at the adult male as he waited outside in his parked Bentley until they saw their favourite teacher walking across the playground and Mark getting out of his vehicle to greet her. They ran away giggling at the thought that Miss Stanley had a boyfriend.

Jean's heart jumped a beat as she spotted Mark. He was apologetic as she drew close to him.

"I am sorry, but I have been missing you and wanted to talk to you. I hope you don't mind. I can give you a lift home, and if you can spare the time, perhaps we could stop for a chat."

"It is good to see you, Mark. How have you been?"

Jean pointed to her own parked car.

"I have to get home to Mother, but If you follow me, we can stop at the café in Bucton and have a quick chat. I have missed you too."

She waited until Mark had climbed back into his car before driving off in front, noting that he walked with a slight limp.

Inside Betty's café in Bucton, she watched him perch uncomfortably on a bar stool and saw him wince.

"Have you hurt yourself, Mark? Did that happen in the quarry?"

"Yes, Jean. About a week ago. I have a gash in my right thigh. Don't concern yourself. It needed a couple of stitches, but it will heal."

"Did you fall over? What happened?"

"One of the crane drivers dropped a load of limestone close to me. A piece flew up and hit me."

"That should not have happened, Mark. You could have been more seriously injured. Safety regulations are in place to protect the working crews. Who was the crane driver, do you know?"

Mark reluctantly admitted that it was her friend Ben.

"We have had a few confrontations lately, Jean. I am not his favourite person. He is always glaring down at me if he sees me in the quarry. I do not think his action was intentional, but he is still passionately in love with you, and jealousy can drive a man to do anything."

Jean was aghast.

"I have told him that though we are good friends, and we have a history together from our youth, I do not love him in the way he wants me to, and we do not have a future together. I told him to find a new girlfriend."

Mark shook his head.

"I do not think that will happen. He is too besotted with you."

"I will have another word with him, Mark, but I suggest that you keep your distance from him. I have never thought of him as a man of violence, and I agree that dropping that load close to you was probably accidental, but you still need to be careful. I noticed how much he had changed when I returned from teaching college. His moods seemed a lot darker."

"Jean, I did not intend to tell you about my injury or who caused it. I wanted you to know that my father suggested that I enrol in one of the Earth Science Institutes or a Geological

Engineering Society to gain more knowledge about the Earth's structure and perhaps earn a degree or a diploma. I am not one for swotting, as you know, but what do you think?"

"That is a good idea, Mark, if you have set your mind on being a geologist. You have had some experience now of fieldwork so apart from pleasing your father you will be able to set your sights higher to fulfil your ambition. I will support you all the way."

Mark sighed.

"What have I let myself in for? Alright, I will go for it if I have your backing. Incidentally, I must apologise for my surliness when I dropped you off at your home after our weekend trip. I was disappointed that I would not be able to see you as much as I would have liked because you wanted to devote any spare time to helping your mother recover her mental health."

Jean smiled.

"I am glad that you understand, Mark. I enjoy your company very much, and we can be together as often as possible, providing it does not interfere with my mother's care. I want you to succeed and not be dependent on your father's allowance. That means, if you will forgive the pun, that you will need to put your nose to the grindstone! Your reward will be my love and respect."

Mark nodded. "I know, Jean. Though I wish that there was an easier way!"

He smiled wryly.

"Why did I have to fall in love with a determined female with such high moral standards? I was having fun before we met."

Jean shook her head.

"No, Mark, you were deceiving yourself. You were wasting your life and lacking self-respect. You say you love me, but you may have said that to all the girls you have met. I know that you have had affairs, but I do not think that you gained much satisfaction from them. I am a normal woman and have my yearnings. Sexual passion is an extreme human emotion, and it dwells within most women and will be felt when they have been aroused and excited by a loving and trusted partner. There is nothing wrong with that, but it generally fades in time, while genuine love is longer lasting, and in the end, more satisfying and rewarding. That is what I want for us, Mark, and I am prepared to wait for it."

To the astonishment of the café owner who was standing behind the counter, Mark slipped off his stool, took one step towards Jean, and kissed her softly on the forehead.

"You are not a normal woman, Jean. You are a remarkable one. I want you, and I need you, but I will wait until you are ready for me."

Chapter 25

Jean returned to school at the beginning of the autumn term and quickly became involved in teaching a class of new pupils. In addition, the female Head asked her to form a new drama group with some of the more senior students, so she had little time to think about Mark and wonder if he had acted on Sir Joshua's suggestion that he enrol in a Geological Research Institute or was still working down in the quarry. She learned the answer to that when he rang her one evening when she was attending to her mother.

"I am doing both," he informed her.

"Two days fieldwork in the open mine and three days studying Earth sciences at a college in Manchester. I am learning quite a lot there and surprisingly find it fascinating."

"Oh, Mark, I am so pleased for you. You must keep going at that. Your father will be thrilled, and so will mine."

"How is your mother, Jean? Can she spare you for an hour or so one evening? I am missing you, and I want to tell you about the college."

"Mark, I miss you too, but I am so busy at school now. Mother is showing some signs of lifting from her depression, but I do not think that I can leave her alone with Dad just yet. Can you give me another week or two? We can always chat on the phone."

Mark sounded dejected.

"Jean, you are making life hard for me! Alright, I will ask you again next week. I may have to console myself with one of my old flames!"

"Don't you dare, Mark Raeburn! I will never forgive you!"

"I am teasing you, Jean. You are the only woman I want and will always want, even though you are a hard taskmaster –or mistress, perhaps I should say."

Mark rang off after getting Jean's assurance that she would spend an evening with him the following weekend. She checked on her mother to make sure that she was comfortable and then joined her father in the lounge. She told him about the conversation with Mark.

"That is good to hear, Jean. He seems to be changing his ways. Obviously, he is very fond of you. I may start thinking of him as a future son-in-law!"

"Dad, I have to admit that I am very attracted to him, but it is too early to think that. He still has to prove that he would be a supportive partner and will agree to my continuation as a schoolteacher after our marriage."

"I think that we have already discussed this, Jean. You know my view. I am an old-fashioned man. Being a wife and mother is a big enough role for any woman. However, that is for you and Mark to work out."

He paused and then added, "As long as you provide grandchildren for your mother and I!"

Chapter 26

Jean received the long-awaited call from Mark the following Friday late afternoon. He apologised for the delay and explained that he had been held up at the college and had only just returned to Punting. Could he pick her up in an hour and take her for an evening meal?

"Yes, Mark, I will like that, and I will be ready."

She checked with her father that he would be at home all evening and quickly showered and changed into the most glamorous dress in her wardrobe. Taking extra care over her hair and make-up, she waited impatiently for Mark's arrival. He nodded his approval when she answered his knock at the cottage door.

"Jean, you look beautiful. No one would take you for a schoolteacher. That is no disrespect to all the ladies in your profession. I will be the envy of every man tonight."

Jean gave him a curtsy.

"Thank you, sir. You look very handsome yourself in your bow tie."

Mark escorted her to his car, sat her inside and fastened her seat belt. Remembering the first time he had tried to do so, and she had forestalled him, she allowed him to lean over and click the belt into place. She placed her right hand over his as he did so and gave him a kiss on the cheek.

Mark's eyes widened in surprise.

"That was very nice! Are you that pleased to see me?"

"Yes, you know I am. It is also a reward for your effort to turn yourself into a respectable citizen."

Mark levered himself into the driving seat.

"Jean, I am only doing this because of you. I would not bother if it was anybody else. I have not listened to anyone since coming out of university, not even my father. You have seen something in me that I did not know was there, and I thank you for that. In fact, I love your confidence in me. It is the reason that I always want to be with you. Incidentally, your perfume is quite intoxicating!"

"It is for special occasions. I do not use it very often."

Mark gazed at her more keenly.

"You consider this to be a special occasion?"

"Of course. It is unlikely that we will get together very often, now that you are studying at Manchester when you are not down in the quarry. It will take you a few months to assimilate all the knowledge of your chosen subjects that you will need to gain the necessary qualifications for a successful career. I will be busy at school, having taken over the drama group, so it may be the end of term before we can get together regularly."

Mark groaned.

"I think that I will need plenty of encouragement from you if I am to finish this course. I am enjoying the studies now, but whether I can continue for the next few months is debatable. I will always be thinking that we could be out enjoying ourselves."

"Mark, you need to make a commitment. I am certain that you have the intelligence to pass all the exams, so all you need is the desire and the motivation. Your love for me should be enough. I will support you all I can, but I will provide criticism as well as praise. You must accept that. It is the way I teach in school. When I first met you, I thought that you were overconfident and too sure of yourself, but now I realise that was a sham. Underneath that smooth-talking exterior is a confused sensitive man who had lost his way. If I thought you were not worth saving, I would not be here."

Mark looked embarrassed at Jean's analysis of his character but did not comment. He switched on the ignition and put the car into gear.

"Let's go! I am hungry, but I also need a drink!"

Chapter 27

Sitting in the lounge bar of the Grand Hotel in Punting forty minutes later, sipping a martini with Mark beside her holding a glass of single malt Irish whisky, and with the evening meal ordered, Jean felt at ease.

"This is very pleasant, Mark. Tell me about your studies at the Institute."

Mark gave Jean quite a detailed account of his geological education. A lot of what he told her about Earth sciences went over her head as he enthused about lithospheres and biospheres, petrology and plate tectonics, but she listened intently and was thrilled that a man who professed no love of history could refer to the planet as it was first formed four billion years ago. With his growing knowledge and newly found enthusiasm, he could eventually become a scientist of renown. The path to success was opening. Jean wanted to hug him.

The evening passed quickly. Mark glanced at his watch.

"It is time I took you home, Cinderella, before you lose a slipper and my car turns into a pumpkin! I have probably bored you to tears, anyway."

"No, no," Jean protested.

"l am so pleased that you may have found your niche. I did not expect you to find it so quickly or this particular field."

Mark leaned forward across the table with a serious expression on his face, and he looked squarely at Jean.

"I have you to thank for all your encouragement. I have needed a push and even a kick on my backside, and you have provided it. I suppose you would not consider a marriage proposal?"

Jean smiled at him mischievously.

"I will think about it, Mark. Ask me again when you have your doctorate!"

She stretched across and kissed him full on his lips.

With the car outside the cottage, Jean unbuckled her seat belt and turned to Mark to plant another kiss on his cheek.

"It's been a lovely evening, Mark. Thank you. Give me a ring tomorrow."

Mark made a move to embrace her. Jean moved away from his outstretched arms and climbed out of the car.

"It is late, and Father will want to get to bed. I must look in on Mother, too. I do love you, but please go home!"

Henry was dozing in his chair when Jean entered the lounge. He yawned and stretched his body. With a tired voice, he asked if she had enjoyed the evening.

"Yes, Dad. Mark hinted at proposing marriage!"

Her father fully opened his eyes at this confession.

"And what was your response?"

"I told him that he must wait a while before putting the question directly. He has to complete his studies first, and there are other issues to discuss, including my teaching career and my responsibility to you and Mother."

Henry waved an impatient hand.

"That is nonsense, Jean! If you really love Mark, you cannot give up your chance of happiness to look after your mother and me. I would not allow it. Nor would your mother if she was in her right mind. I am sure that if we needed urgent medical attention, we would get it from our local surgery. Besides, I have told you that we both need a grandchild to cuddle in our old age."

"I understand that, Dad, but please give me time. Let me get you into bed, and then I will see to Mother."

Chapter 28

Mark rang Jean the next evening as promised and asked if he could call in and chat to her.

Henry was reading the *Mining Gazette* when his daughter answered the knock on the door. He rose to his feet and offered his hand to the visitor.

"Hello, Mark. It's good to see you. Come on in. I know you want to talk to my daughter, so I will retire to my room so that you can chat privately. Jean will call me when you are ready to leave."

Mark stepped forward and shook the proffered hand.

"Thank you, sir. It is good to see you again."

Henry smiled.

"I have heard good reports of your study at the Institute and that you are actively engaged in the quarry. I am pleased for your sake."

"I am learning quite a lot, Mr Stanley, and I am grateful for your personal input."

"Good, then keep at it. I will see you later."

As soon as her father left the room, Mark scooped Jean into his arms. She responded to his kiss lovingly. After a passionate couple of minutes, Jean took a deep breath.

"Please take a seat, Mark. I would like to discuss one or two things before I agree to marry you. There are a couple of important conditions that you must accept. First, despite some protest from my father last night, I cannot leave home until my mother's mental health has improved, nor can I leave Father to look after her even if she accepts his help. He is reasonably well at present, but at his age illness can strike at any time. Secondly, you know that I want to continue with my school teaching, and you must agree to that. I can only do so with your full support. The other condition, which you already know, is that you must complete your studies and not give up halfway through because you have lost interest."

Mark nodded.

"I love you, Jean, so I will agree to all your terms. Your happiness is very important to me, but please do not keep me waiting too long. Can we consider ourselves engaged, at least?"

He delved into his pocket and pulled out a small black velvet box. He held it out to Jean and motioned her to open it. Inside was a diamond solitaire set on a 22-carat gold band. "Will you wear it until a wedding band can be added? I am not sure if it is the right size, but we can get it altered if need be."

Jean tried it on the third finger of her right hand. It fitted perfectly. She held out her hand to show Mark, her face shining with pleasure and love.

He grinned broadly.

"Please, Miss, can I ask a question?"

Jean smiled back.

"Yes, of course, if it is important."

"Oh, it is, Miss, very important. Can I have a kiss, please?"

Chapter 29

Three weeks later, on a cold and frosty Monday morning, Ben Haywood climbed into his cab in the crane he operated. He was in a very black mood and had a heavy hangover, which was the result of spending the weekend drinking in the Pig and Whistle with his mind on Jean and her suitor Mark Raeburn. He was consumed with hatred for a man who had robbed him of all hope that Jean and he would spend the rest of their lives together.

Ben had been devastated when Jean elected to go to teacher training college in London, and he spent those three years in abject misery waiting for her return. When she did so, he found that she had changed. They were still friends, but she had grown and matured beyond an academic level that he could not match. She had told him that her ambition was to follow a teaching career, and marriage to him or anybody else was not part of her dream. He took to drink after that and spent his days idling until he was offered the crane driver's job in the quarry. He agreed to take the post because he knew that Jean's father worked there. It was not much of a link, but it made him feel closer to her. He reluctantly accepted that loose association until Mark Raeburn appeared on the scene and took an interest in her.

Ben had tried unsuccessfully to warn off the son of the quarry owner by dropping a load of limestone close to him, but that ended with a strong hint of a dismissal from the site manager. Since that failed episode, he had tried to provoke Raeburn into arguments that would culminate in his love rival abandoning his fieldwork in the quarry. He thought that he had achieved that when Mark failed to show up for work until he discovered that his rival was studying in Manchester on certain days of the week.

Ben took a swig from a hip flask of whisky that was hidden in the back pocket of his dungarees and reflected on his youth. Jean and he had been almost inseparable then until Maisie Parsons had caught them together in the river. Well, he had dealt with her. He had gone down to the river, as he often did, to remember the joyous times when he and Jean had swum together when he saw Maisie spying on another young courting couple. It enraged him that she was still up to her shameful tricks years later. He recalled his and Jean's embarrassment at the accusations aimed at them then and, in his anger, picked up a heavy stone and hit the postmistress on the back of her head. She fell forward soundlessly unconscious on the riverbank.

He studied her bloody scalp for a moment before turning and walking away, leaving the young couple unaware of the brutal incident that had taken place so close behind them. Hearing two days later that Maisie had been found drowned in the river surprised him. He presumed that she had rolled down the bank and fallen into the water, still unconscious. Well, good riddance! At least she would not be spying on anybody else. He had been one of the Bucton residents questioned later by police, but he had denied that he had been anywhere near the river on the day it was estimated that she had met her death.

Ben looked at the ground below. He saw the site manager standing with Mark Raeburn, watching as quarrymen were preparing to blast a chunk of limestone rock out of the cavern wall, drilling holes in order to insert sticks of gelignite. Once the fuses were lit, the miners would move to a safe distance away from the tons of rock that would be hurled outwards. It was Ben's job to gather up all the limestone with his crane and take it where it could be examined for its mineral content. He sat and waited to make his move. Here was another opportunity to get rid of the man who plagued his life.

Chapter 30

Jean was in the school gymnasium taking a physical exercise class when she received a message that the Headmistress wanted to see her. She put the class in charge of the senior girl and hurried to the Head's study, worried that some calamity had occurred in the cottage which involved one or both her parents. She burst into the room to find the Head standing at her desk, holding a telephone.

"It's your father, Jean. There has been an accident at the quarry."

Jean's thoughts immediately flew to Mark. She knew that he would be in the quarry that day. She took the telephone from her senior and anxiously gasped into it.

"What has happened, Dad? Who has been hurt? Is Mark alright?"

She heard her father's grave tone in reply.

"There was an explosion during blasting. Some of the men were injured, but Mark is alright. The most seriously injured was the crane driver, Ben Haywood, who has been taken to hospital. I know that he is an old friend of yours so I thought that I should tell you. I am not sure that he will survive."

"Oh, Dad, that is awful news, but thanks. With the head's permission, I will drive straight to the hospital."

Standing beside her, the Headmistress nodded. Jean put the receiver down, grateful that Mark had not been hurt but now concerned about Ben. She hurried to her car and drove at a fast pace to the local medical centre. Admitted into the Intensive Care Unit, she found Ben lying motionless, wrapped up in a bed with his eyes closed. The nurse standing by looked at Jean and shook her head. Jean bent down and gently touched Ben's hand, which was slightly protruding from the blanket. His eyes opened slowly and gazed up at Jean's face. He appeared to recognise her, for he tried to turn his hand to hold her fingers. A brief smile lit up his bloodied features for an instant before he closed his eyes again.

Jean sat with him for a while, but there was no other movement. Later, she spoke to a senior doctor who informed her that the patient had suffered a fractured skull and had broken his spine. There was nothing that could be done for him but administer morphine and make his last moments comfortable.

Jean drove back to the school, but noting her pale teary face, the Headmistress told her to go home. Her father gave her more details of the tragic accident. Apparently, one of the blasting charges had exploded later than the others when it was presumed that they had gone off together, and Ben had moved closer to remove some of the ejected limestone. A large piece of rock had catapulted violently out of the quarry face and smashed against the crane. Ben was thrown out of his cab and landed heavily backwards on the rock, sustaining his injuries. Fortunately, other quarrymen, including Mark and the site manager, received only cuts and bruises from smaller chunks of debris.

Jean rang the hospital later that day and was sadly informed that Ben had passed away shortly after she had left the ITU. She asked if his parents had been contacted and was told that they had received the sad news.

Jean decided to take a couple of days' leave of absence from school so that she could call on them and express her sympathy. Mark also rang her to give his assurance that he had not been badly hurt in the delayed explosion. He expressed his sympathy at Ben's death, which warmed Jean's heart, knowing how much he had been provoked by her old friend because of his relationship with her. It pleased her even more that he agreed to accompany her on her visit to Ben's parents. It proved that beneath the charm and bravado lay a sensitive and compassionate man.

Chapter 31

Ben's funeral took place on a grey and cheerless day appropriate to the occasion. There were few mourners except for Jean, accompanied to her surprise by Mark, and Ben's elderly parents. One or two quarrymen whom Ben had not offended were also present. Jean reflected on how much he had changed since the carefree days of their youth. His unrequited love for her had made him a bitter, angry man. She wondered how different he would have been if she had accepted his marriage proposal. She was not responsible for his anger against Mark, nor for her lack of passion in her rejection of his sexual advances, but she owed him for his friendship at a tender age when she may have needed his protection against possible abusers. She thought about her relationship with Mark. He knew that she loved him and wanted to spend the rest of her life with him, but he also needed to know that their marriage would not be sexually inhibited. She was determined to tell him so the next time they met in private.

At the cemetery gates, Jean said goodbye to the other mourners and drove Ben's parents back to their home, where they thanked her for paying the funeral bill. Mark had offered to pay towards it, even though he had been a victim of Ben's animosity, but Jean told him it was unnecessary. She also asked Mark if he wanted to go back to the cottage with her, but he declined, telling her that he had a thesis to write that required handing in to the Institute the next day. It was possible he may have to stay there for a few days because his geological studies were reaching a critical stage.

Jean was disappointed by this news and realised that her hormones were all over the place. It seemed as if the tables had been turned on her. Suddenly she knew that she required Mark's comforting presence to bring calmness back into her life. She stretched up and kissed him, wishing him well in his studies and telling him to ring her whenever he could. It seemed that their intimate chat would have to wait.

One week later, her father suffered a mild stroke while up in his hut on the lip of the quarry. He remained stable enough to send a garbled message to the site manager, who quickly arranged for an ambulance to transport Henry to Punting General Hospital. Jean, back at school, had to ask for more cover so that she could attend the hospital. She was told by the heart specialist that her father's heart and main arteries were in reasonably good shape for a man of his age, and the stroke had probably been caused by the stress of observing the tragic accident down in the quarry which had resulted in the death of the crane driver. Nevertheless, a stent was inserted in a partly blocked main artery, and he was discharged with the recommendation of complete rest. At some later stage, he may require the fitment of a pacemaker.

Surprisingly, Ann was the first at the door to greet the ambulance when it arrived with Henry. She watched as he was placed in a wheelchair and brought into the sitting room. She thanked the ambulancemen for the heart and blood thinning medication and, with their departure, gazed directly at her husband.

She asked, "How are you, Henry?"

It was the first time that she had spoken to him in months.

Henry stared at her and said in a puzzled tone, "I am alright, my dear. It is nice to be home."

Jean was also perplexed, though delighted by her mother's changed attitude. What had caused it? She had been receiving counselling for a long time, but it had not caused any positive result. It seemed that Henry's stroke had suddenly raised alarm. Ann had wanted to know the seriousness of his condition and whether it would prove fatal. That seemed to show that despite all her indifference to him and her continual rejection, she still cared for him. She had used him as a scapegoat for the loss of their baby son because she had to blame someone. She could not blame herself or God, so she chose her husband. It is an adage that when you are hurt, you tend to blame the person closest to you, and in this instance, it was Henry. That was fine while he was alive, and she could punish him, but it was a different matter if he was not.

Jean suddenly realised that her mother still loved her father and needed him in her life. That thought thrilled Jean because she had always wanted that loving bond restored. Ann's physical health was good, and her depression was easing. Caring for her husband during his convalescence would be therapeutic for them both. Henry, still in love with his wife despite her coldness, would be very happy to receive her loving attention. Jean returned to school feeling almost pleased that her father had suffered a mild stroke. It was the catalyst that may finally heal her mother's anguish.

Chapter 32

Jean's attention turned to Mark. His father had informed him that he had considered his studies were more important than the manual work in the quarry. He wanted his son to continue the course at the Manchester Institute and then move on to another geological college in order to obtain a top degree. Jean had approved of that progression even though it meant that she would see less of Mark. Much as she required his presence while she was feeling sensitive at the death of Ben, it was important that her fiancé gain all the necessary qualifications that would provide them with a comfortable lifestyle independent of financial assistance from parents. In the meantime, she would focus on training her young students to reach their full potential.

Weeks went by. Henry was able to stroll around his garden with the aid of a stout cane, with Ann watching his every move. He had accepted that he would not be able to continue with his observation of the groundwork in the little hut, but he was happy that Ann was back caring for him and attending to his needs.

Jean was also relieved and thankful that her parents were no longer detached from each other. They were not yet back to the loving relationship that had existed before Simon's death, but she was hopeful that given time it would be. Ann's melancholia had lifted; it seemed that she had finally come to accept the realisation that their baby son would not have recovered from meningitis at his young age. Henry had played no part in his loss.

Mark telephoned one evening when Jean was closeted in her bedroom, happy that her parents were sitting close together in the lounge conversing with each other.

"I have been given a week's respite before the next period of study. I am coming down to Punting to chat with my father, so what evening is most convenient to drop in to you without disturbing your parents?"

Jean laughed.

"Don't be silly, Mark. You can come in any time. We are engaged, so you do not need to ask permission! My parents are communicating with each other now, and I have told Mother that you are studying Geology. I do not think that she will be quite so standoffish with you. Incidentally, it is my birthday at the end of next week. Perhaps we could book a foursome to have a celebratory meal in Punting?"

"That would be marvellous, Jean! Is your dad capable of going out? I will be very glad to book a table for us. Hopefully, we can have some time together alone after that!"

"Father is making good progress, Mark, so I think that he will enjoy getting out of the house, especially if Mother is sitting beside him."

"Fine, Jean. I will make the arrangements. What would you like as a birthday present?"

"Just being with you will be sufficient, Mark. I am missing you."

Henry was delighted at the thought of a meal out with his wife and daughter and looked forward to a chat with Mark. Ann was uncertain of her feelings about meeting her daughter's new betrothed, but she was curious to see how much change, if any, there had been in his previous casual behaviour.

Chapter 33

Entering her classroom on the morning of her 26th birthday, Jean was surprised to find several greeting cards on her desk, while across the blackboard, the message *Happy Birthday, Miss Stanley* had been scribbled in large letters, accompanied by the signatures of the pupils. Jean was delighted by this show of affection. It was her reward for the careful and patient attention she had paid to everyone in the class, motivating them to get fully involved in every subject she taught. It also confirmed her desire to continue teaching for as long as she was able.

That evening, having joyfully greeted Mark on his arrival at the cottage, Jean sat beside him as he drove to the hotel where he had booked the evening meal. In the Bentley's rear seats, her parents were dressed in their best attire.

Inside the dining room of the hotel, the central table held a large bouquet of red roses. A silver bucket holding a magnum of champagne stood close to it on the immaculate white tablecloth. Beside Jean's place was a small package with a card attached. It read *Happy Birthday, Jean*. Three of the diners stood and gazed at the table as the fourth stood back and observed their amazed reaction.

"It's lovely, Mark," Jean acknowledged as they all took their seats.

"You have been busy! Thank you."

She picked up the package and opened it. Inside was an amethyst amulet, its purple colouring sparkling in the light of the chandelier overhead.

"It's beautiful, Mark. Thank you."

"It is also appropriate, Jean. It is made of silica or quartz, the semi-precious mineral found in ancient rock all around the world. It is regarded as a good luck charm, protecting you against evil spirits. This particular piece came from Brazil, I understand."

Jean gazed lovingly at Mark as her parents admired the amethyst.

"Then I will always wear it. Thank you again."

The sumptuous five-course meal was appetising enough to satisfy the most discerning diner, though Jean was too excited with Mark sitting beside her to do it justice. Her good health and happiness were toasted with the champagne. Henry caused laughter with his comment that the bubbles tickled his nose, and Mark ordered a glass of single malt Glenfiddich for him, which appealed more to his taste.

Jean was pleased that the two men had formed a good relationship which ordained well for the future, while Ann seemed to have lost some of her former hostility towards Sir Joshua's son. She seemed happy to engage in conversation with him, mentioning her own childhood growing up in Derbyshire. The return drive to Wisteria Cottage at the end of the evening was accomplished in a collective spirit of bonhomie.

Chapter 34

Later that evening, with her parents retired for the night, Jean became more serious and broached the subject which had occupied her mind since Ben's death. She discarded the notion that the champagne had gone to her head, but she opened the conversation delicately.

"Mark, it may be a year or two before we can get married because I want you to complete all your studies and be rewarded with academic honours. During that period, there will be a temptation for us to enter a more intimate relationship because of our love for each other. You are a passionate man, and I have a desire for you that will not be easy to quench. However, my parents are quite old-fashioned, and I was brought up to believe that sex before marriage is immoral. Living with them as I do, I would feel very uncomfortable with them realising that we were intimate before we made our wedding vows. I hope you understand that. From my experience with Ben and his impassioned display when he proposed to me, I know how hard it is for men to hold their frustrations in check, and it certainly caused a change in his personality that surprised me. I think that you have a far stronger character and can control those feelings. I know you have had your flings in the past, but they were only temporary urges. The love and desire we share goes far deeper than those and will always be part of our married life."

Mark had listened in silence and hesitated before replying.

"I am very pleased to hear that, Jean. I am not going to deny that I am eager to have a full physical relationship with you, but I have never forced myself on any woman. I love you, but what we do sexually must be completely consensual. I have previously told you that I will wait until you are ready for me. That commitment still stands, though perhaps it is fortunate for us that we will both be fully occupied in the next year or so; you with your schoolwork and myself endeavouring to gain the degrees I will need. Thank goodness that, at the moment, I am absorbed in everything I am being taught and even more enthusiastic to extend my knowledge. It will not keep my mind entirely off you because I will always be desiring you, but I will try to keep my passion in check."

He kissed her full on the lips.

"I shall rely on you to keep me in order, my love. You may need the discipline you use in school!"

"I am not a strict disciplinarian, Mark. I prefer to use gentle persuasion, so I hope that will be effective on you! If you keep looking at me the way you do sometimes, I may need to force myself to apply some self-restraint!"

Chapter 35

During the harsh months of winter that followed, Henry was glad that he was not working up in the hut, which had been abandoned and emptied of its furniture and telecommunication apparatus. It had looked increasingly ramshackle, being battered by strong winds. One night in March, a violent storm broke over Bucton Tor, which led to its complete collapse. Savage gusts tore away the last of the timber hut's foundations, and it slowly toppled over the lip of the quarry. It plummeted to the ground and smashed completely to pieces. Fortunately, no workmen stood nearby.

Henry was sorry to hear of the hut's demise, but Sir Joshua was not concerned. It was surplus to requirements, and he had only left it in situ for his semi-retired worker to have some part-time activity while he was recovering from his lung surgery. With Henry and his wife restored to their affectionate relationship, there was no need for the hut. With spring arriving, his former employee could spend time in the cottage garden, leisurely growing vegetables and flowers. His heart surgeon had recommended that method of gentle exercise.

Jean had returned to school with the relief that her parents were no longer disconnected. It meant that she could spend more time outside the set curriculum stimulating her young pupils to further their academic knowledge and succeed in their exams. Mark was in a similar situation in the Geology Institute in Manchester, though progressing well. He had joined several other institutions that taught geotechnical engineering and was preparing for his degree. Jean was thrilled to hear that news because it showed that he had the ability and the will to complete his studies and be worthy of her love. Her mind turned to the prospect of an earlier marriage than she had anticipated, and her heart leaped with joy. She told him so in their next telephone conversation.

"Mark, I am so thrilled for you. You are exceeding all my expectations! I want to plan our wedding now. I love you so much that I do not want to wait much longer to be in your arms!"

"Jean, I am anxious for us to be married, too, but I have several months' study yet, so we may have to wait until I get my Chartered Geologist status. I have been studying sedimentary rock, since most of my father's quarry and most of Derbyshire is made up of limestone and sandstone, but there are so many types I need to understand to complete my education. I want to study marine biology, too, because the Peak District was once a huge lagoon, not as it is now."

Jean was astonished by Mark's new-found enthusiasm but delighted by it.

"That is wonderful, Mark. I think geology should be a key subject in schools as everyone should learn about our planet Earth and its structure. I shall endeavour to teach my young pupils about it so they realise how much damage humans have caused to our natural environment over the years. It is vital that we do not use up all its resources so that we do not lose the wildlife that depends on it. Humans will suffer, too, unless we act to preserve them."

"Climatology may be my next subject, Jean. I hope to get a break in two weeks so we can further discuss the dangers that may lie ahead unless we all change our habits. We can set an approximate date for our wedding then."

Chapter 36

Winter turned into spring. Harmony reigned in the Stanley household. Henry had fully recovered from his stroke and was busy planting vegetables in his garden with Ann beside him ensuring that he did not exert himself. Jean was happily occupied by the planning of the wedding, with a date set for mid-July during the school summer break. Mark had passed three of his Geology exams with honours and was preparing for two more which would give him his Chartered Geology status. He told Jean that he was anxious to gain degrees in Lithostratigraphy and Lithesome, which involved the study of sedimentary rock layers that form most of Derbyshire and, more pertinently, Bucton quarry. With those achievements under his belt, Mark felt that he would have earned the respect of his peer group and dumbfounded all his critics. Moreover, it would satisfy Jean that he had the strength of character and the commitment to deal with any crisis that may crop up in the future. Jean, always certain in her mind that Mark was the man she wanted as her husband, was thrilled beyond measure that her faith in him had been justified, and she pressed on eagerly with her wedding plans.

Six months later, with those further academic successes confirmed, Jean and Mark were married at the parish church in Punting. Among the congregation were the bridegroom's parents, Sir Joshua and Lady Mary Raeburn; Mark's Aunt Beatrice, beaming with pride; Henry and Ann Stanley, also observing their daughter's union with love and joy, and multiple friends and neighbours, including teaching staff and senior pupils from Bucton Primary School and quarrymen

with their families. Outside the church after the service, a group of Jean's class students in freshly pressed school uniform formed a guard of honour for the newlyweds as they headed for the carriage that would whisk them away to the reception hotel.

The honeymoon was spent in Barbados, where Jean not only proved her passionate nature to her new husband but her sense of humour, entering the bridal suite on their first night with a mischievous smile and a cane in her hand. It was not needed.

Eighteen months later, Jean presented Mark with twin daughters, who were instantly named Faith and Hope. Both sets of grandparents were thrilled with the twin girls and promptly offered to babysit at those times when Jean and Mark were actively engaged in their chosen careers. Two years later, when Jean delivered a baby boy, Ann Stanley was ecstatic as she stood at the christening font and heard her grandson named Mark Henry Simon Raeburn. Her eyes brimming with joyful tears, she cradled the infant in her arms when Jean passed him down to her and then pressed his small body close to her chest, reluctant to let him go. Any remaining evidence of melancholia or mental instability vanished, never to return.

Epilogue

After nursing the three children through babyhood, Jean returned to teaching, leaving them safely in the hands of Ann and Henry and a governess. Eventually, she took over as Head of School and served with distinction in that post for many years before retirement. Mark became a senior lecturer in Environmental Studies and received further awards with his knowledge of fossils and other organisms that formed the structure of rocks over the centuries.

No longer in need of his father's allowance, he became financially independent, but as a reward for turning his life around, Sir Joshua had a large family home built in Hope Valley with an attached annexe for the use of Jean's parents. Mark and Jean lived happily there while educating their children in the value of positive thinking. Their twin daughters were a constant reminder that Faith and Hope are sustaining elements when trouble strikes and the future looks uncertain.

www.ingramcontent.com/pod-product-compliance
Lightning Source LLC
Chambersburg PA
CBHW022040170626
46808CB00003B/1292